9/01

LIGHT-GATHERING POEMS

Here are some other Edge Books from Henry Holt you will enjoy:

The Beautiful Days of My Youth: My Six Months in Auschwitz and Plaszow
by Ana Novac
translated from the French by George Newman

Cool Salsa: Bilingual Poems on Growing Up Latino in the United States
edited by Lori M. Carlson

Earth-Shattering Poems
edited by Liz Rosenberg

Forbidden Love: The Secret History of Mixed-Race America
by Gary B. Nash

Hit the Nerve: New Voices of the American Theater
edited by Stephen Vincent Brennan

The Invisible Ladder: An Anthology of Contemporary American Poems for Young Readers
edited by Liz Rosenberg

The Long Season of Rain
by Helen Kim

One Bird
by Kyoko Mori

Remix: Conversations with Immigrant Teenagers
by Marina Budhos

Shizuko's Daughter
by Kyoko Mori

A Way Out of No Way: Writings About Growing Up Black in America
edited by Jacqueline Woodson

We Are Witnesses: The Diaries of Five Teenagers Who Died in the Holocaust
by Jacob Boas

We're Alive and Life Goes On: A Theresienstadt Diary
by Eva Roubíčková
translated from the German by Zaia Alexander

LIGHT-GATHERING POEMS

EDITED BY LIZ ROSENBERG

HENRY HOLT AND COMPANY • NEW YORK

Wholehearted thanks go to my editor, Marc Aronson, generous guiding light; and to the Herculean help given by his assistants, Laurel Girvan, Chris Lee, and David Rohlfing, without whom I would still be sweeping out the Aegean Stables. Loving thanks to my husband, David, who made copies in the middle of the night; to our son, Eli, the young computer expert; to Cheryl DeLuke, who makes so much of our daily life possible; to Debbie, who keeps the house organized; and to friends and students, who made brilliant suggestions. Gratitude to the many permissions editors who make the anthologist's life a bit easier. And to the poets—of course!

Henry Holt and Company, LLC
Publishers since 1866
115 West 18th Street
New York, New York 10011

Henry Holt is a registered trademark of Henry Holt and Company, LLC

Library of Congress Cataloging-in-Publication Data
Light-gathering poems / edited by Liz Rosenberg
p.   cm.—(Edge books)
Includes bibliographical references and index.
1. Young adult poetry.   I. Rosenberg, Liz.   II. Series.
PN6109.97 .L54 2000   808.81—dc21   99-049231

ISBN 0-8050-6223-8
First Edition—2000
Printed in the United States of America on acid-free paper. ∞
1   3   5   7   9   10   8   6   4   2

Design by Debbie Glasserman

To the Slonim family, lighting up the city of Binghamton,
who taught me about tikkun olam

To all bright shards everywhere

CONTENTS

This collection began as a sister-book—a companion, if you will—to an earlier anthology I'd edited, called *Earth-Shattering Poems*. While those poems focused on turmoil—first death, first broken heart, the endless devastation of war—*Light-Gathering Poems* was intended as a healing answer, poems that in one way or another turn toward the light.

Of course, like all books, this one took on a life of its own. It is still intended to be a celebratory and comforting book, which does *not* mean it is all laughter and cheeriness. Sometimes one only comes to the light through a dark journey. An old saying goes: The greatest ascent is preceded by the greatest descent.

I have tried to choose poems for this collection that do "gather light"—either literally or figuratively. (Or both at once.) Some I chose for their beauty ("Stopping by Woods on a Snowy Evening," my favorite poem as a child), or a golden sunniness, like Wordsworth's famous poem about the daffodils. Some are about simple kinds of happiness, like finding the same smooth stone in your pocket twice in one day, in Das Lanzillotti's "On Days Like This," or the simple kindness of Christina Rossetti's "Hurt No Living Thing," or Langston Hughes's sheer determination to laugh in the face of his own blues. The reader will find an African-American freedom song, a psalm from King David, and many love poems, both ancient and modern.

Certain poems were included in this collection because they express pleasure, or gratitude; the joy of Frank O'Hara's exuberant "Having a Coke with You," as well as the ecstasy of the first whirling dervish, Rumi, a thirteenth-century poet. I've looked for poems that express courage; praise; *vivas* like Gary Soto's at the instant he's mistakenly chased from his own country. The Russian poet Tsvetaeva expresses relief that she can be sloppy and outspoken, and no longer feels "suffocating waves" every time her old beloved walks by. (Though I wonder if her poem may not be brave whistling in the dark.) But then, many poems found their way into this book on nothing more than hope, as in Shelley's great line, "If Winter comes, can Spring be far behind?" What a hopeful way to look at the dead of winter!

Though the reader will find many images of light here—moonlight, sunlight, rainbows, and everything in between—I don't mean the title to be taken too literally. Light doesn't equal white, anymore than black equals darkness and despair. These images have created great harm for too long. The African-American poet Angelina Weld Grimké gives us a blackness "Slim and still, / Against a gold, gold sky . . . A black finger / Pointing upwards." It is a vision of waiting, growing, aspiring; what the novelist John Gardner called "divine stubbornness." There are many ways to gather light. The poet Rilke thinks of us all as falling, yet held up by invisible hands that sustain even the falling. William Stafford advises us on "Learning How to Lose," and Ruth Stone remembers the wind shaking her sleep, "Like a definition of love, / Saying, this is the moment, / Here, now." The poet Billy Collins celebrates a moth; Frost, a butterfly; Christina Rossetti, gnats and beetles, even "harmless worms that creep."

All poets must train themselves to look, and to see. These poets have gone a step further, to look toward some brightness, some way of rescue, hope, or comfort. Our great American poet Walt Whitman sees his immortal soul as fragile as a spider's single thread, yet insurpassably strong, an "anchor." The Japanese poet Issa reminds us that even the snail can climb Mount Fuji, "but slowly, slowly." Small creatures, small moments. These things are natural objects of attention to young readers, who, for one thing, can still remember what it's like to be short and humble. I have often thought the great virtue of youth is not its beauty, but its hope.

I once had a young student who kept what she called "a happy journal," to remind herself that good things happened every day, even if it was nothing better than eating an ice cream cone. These poets also look hard but hopefully at the world: "looking to love" as Juliet tells her Romeo. As a child, often depressed, often lonely and nervous and feeling hopelessly gawky, I loved poetry not only for its music but also for its hints of possibility. The old-time children's poets, such as Robert Louis Stevenson, used language like "How do you like to go up in a swing, / Up in the air so blue? / Oh, I do think it the pleasantest thing / Ever a child can do!"—which would very likely turn my son's stomach, but which I considered as exotic as the language of elves.

It may be that poetry and possibility are inextricably linked, partly because of its music. As the comic Steve Martin says, it isn't easy to be pompous or miserable while playing the banjo. Rhyme promises the hope of other, deeper connections between things, as do similes and metaphors. This is like that. You feel as I felt.

I hope that any one of these poems might serve as a reminder of our own best possibilities, lift us from a black mood, "save some part of a day I had rued," to quote Robert Frost. There are always acts of love and kindness, of justice and charity, remembrance and hope. Such light-gatherings are recorded in poetry as old as the psalms and as new as that of the newest poet in this book, Kate Schmitt, who tosses a penny in an imaginary wishing well, and remarks: "After I've thrown it I lie / unconcerned. These things take time."

At the end of my introduction to *Earth-Shattering Poems* I mentioned a favorite idea in the oldest Hebrew texts that "we were all once part of God, but that we somehow broke and scattered from that divine source." This same belief looks at each individual as a kernel, or shard of light, capable of growing and joining with others to create greater and brighter light. The act of putting ourselves together again—as Humpty Dumpty could not—is known as *tikkun olam*, making the world whole.

The organization of this book, readers will notice, is alphabetical. This emphasizes the notion that each poet here is a "shard" of light forming a greater whole. There is something mysterious about the way a series of small brilliants light up an entire night sky, and these poems, too, form remarkable constellations. Certain themes appear and reappear, one poem may seem to speak to another—as indeed poets *do* speak to one another, across ages and vast distances. Hopefully, the extensive biographies at the back of this book will make some of those conversations even clearer, for there are connections between what may seem at first glance like the most unlikely poets—the Irish poet Yeats and the Indian poet Tagore; William Blake and William Wordsworth and Allen Ginsberg; and so on. Thanks to the lucky chances of the alphabet, the very first poem of the book is a song about escape from slavery into freedom; the very last tells how songmakers will find a special place waiting for them in heaven.

By holding our particular piece up to the light, holding ourselves up to the light, we do our part toward repairing what is shattered. It is in that spirit that this book is affectionately offered.

LIGHT-GATHERING POEMS

AFRICAN-AMERICAN ANONYMOUS POET *(1800s)*

Follow the drinking gourd,
Follow the drinking gourd,
For the old man is a waitin' for to carry you to freedom,
Follow the drinking gourd.

When the sun comes up and the first quail calls,
Follow the drinking gourd.
The old man is a waitin' for to carry you to freedom,
Follow the drinking gourd.

Now the river bank'll make a mighty good road,
The dead trees will show you the way.
Left foot, peg foot, travelin' on,
Follow the drinking gourd.

Now the river ends between two hills,
Follow the drinking gourd.
There's another river on the other side,
Follow the drinking gourd.

CHARLES BAUDELAIRE   *(1821–1867)*

. . . One morning I woke up cranky, sad, tired out from my own idleness, and pushed, it seemed to me, to do something grand, a brilliant act; and I opened the window, alas! . . .

The first person I noticed in the street was a glazier, whose piercing, discordant cry rose up to me through the heavy, filthy Parisian air. It would be impossible to explain just why I took for this man a sudden, despotic hatred.

"—Hey! Hey!" I called for him to come up. And I reflected, not without a certain glee, that since my room was up six steep flights of stairs, the man would have some trouble climbing up and turning sharp corners with his fragile merchandise.

Finally he appeared: I examined all of his window panes curiously, and said, "What? You have no colored panes? No rose-colored glass, no red, blue, no magical panes, no panes of Paradise? What impudence! how dare you parade around the poor neighborhoods without one single pane of glass to make life beautiful!" And I pushed him toward the stairs where he tottered and grumbled.

I advanced toward my balcony and seized a small pot of flowers, and when the man reappeared at the doorway below, I let fall my engine of war straight on the back edge of his stack; the shock sent him tumbling, so that he managed to break the rest of his poor moveable fortune with the shattering noise of a crystal palace struck by lightning.

And, drunk on my own madness, I cried furiously, "Make life beautiful! make life beautiful!"

Translated from the French by Liz Rosenberg

STEVEN BAUER   *(b. 1948)*

Seven-thirty, last weekend in April,
the sun, like a laggard child, still thumbs
the greening branches
to see how new the world's become.
In this light it's hard to admit so little
has changed. *Maria,* I say, *kiss me.*
When she does, I give myself up
to the pollen
falling from the light-streaked clouds,
tulips holding their white chalices open
to the air. I remember that first evening

I was freed after supper,
amazed by the extra light,
the flat planes of houses aflame
with a radiance I'd never notice again.
The moon hung in the sky, a pale promise.
I hid beside the house, the maple
with its new leaves, green stars
gathering the darkness,
my mother on the red brick steps
cupping her mouth and I thought

*I have light, I have light
in my pockets, I'll save it.*

TO A DARK GIRL

GWENDOLYN B. BENNETT   *(1902–1981)*

I love you for your brownness
And the rounded darkness of your breast.
I love you for the breaking sadness in your voice
And shadows where your wayward eye-lids rest.
Something of old forgotten queens
Lurks in the lithe abandon of your walk
And something of the shackled slave
Sobs in the rhythm of your talk.

Oh, little brown girl, born for sorrow's mate,
Keep all you have of queenliness,
Forgetting that you once were slave,
And let your full lips laugh at Fate!

ETERNITY

WILLIAM BLAKE   *(1757–1827)*

He who binds to himself a joy
Does the wingéd life destroy
But he who kisses the joy as it flies
Lives in eternity's sun rise.

ELIZABETH BARRETT BROWNING   *(1806–1861)*

How do I love thee? Let me count the ways.
I love thee to the depth and breadth and height
My soul can reach, when feeling out of sight
For the ends of Being and ideal Grace.
I love thee to the level of everyday's
Most quiet need, by sun and candle-light.
I love thee freely, as men strive for Right;
I love thee purely, as they turn from Praise.
I love thee with the passion put to use
In my old griefs, and with my childhood's faith.
I love thee with a love I seemed to lose
With my lost saints—I love thee with the breath,
Smiles, tears, of all my life!—and, if God choose,
I shall but love thee better after death.

From *Sonnets from the Portuguese*

SHE WALKS IN BEAUTY

GEORGE GORDON, LORD BYRON *(1788–1823)*

She walks in beauty, like the night
   Of cloudless climes and starry skies;
And all that's best of dark and bright
   Meet in her aspect and her eyes:
Thus mellowed to that tender light
   Which heaven to gaudy day denies.

One shade the more, one ray the less,
   Had half impaired the nameless grace
Which waves in every raven tress,
   Or softly lightens o'er her face;
Where thoughts serenely sweet express
   How pure, how dear their dwelling place.

And on that cheek, and o'er that brow,
   So soft, so calm, yet eloquent,
The smiles that win, the tints that glow,
   But tell of days in goodness spent,
A mind at peace with all below,
   A heart whose love is innocent!

BROKEN AND BROKEN . . .

CHOSU   *(dates unknown)*

Broken and broken
Again on the sea, the moon
So easily mends.

Translated from the Japanese by Harry Behn

SAMUEL TAYLOR COLERIDGE   *(1772–1834)*

Dear Babe, that sleepest cradled by my side,
Whose gentle breathings, heard in this deep calm,
Fill up the intersperséd vacancies
And momentary pauses of the thought!
My babe so beautiful! it thrills my heart
With tender gladness, thus to look at thee,
And think that thou shalt learn far other lore,
And in far other scenes! For I was reared
In the great city, pent 'mid cloisters dim,
And saw nought lovely but the sky and stars.
But *thou*, my babe! shalt wander like a breeze
By lakes and sandy shores, beneath the crags
Of ancient mountain, and beneath the clouds,
Which image in their bulk both lakes and shores
And mountain crags: so shalt thou see and hear
The lovely shapes and sounds intelligible
Of that eternal language, which thy God
Utters, who from eternity doth teach
Himself in all, and all things in himself.
Great universal Teacher! he shall mold
Thy spirit, and by giving make it ask.

Therefore all seasons shall be sweet to thee,
Whether the summer clothe the general earth
With greenness, or the redbreast sit and sing
Betwixt the tufts of snow on the bare branch
Of mossy apple tree, while the nigh thatch
Smokes in the sun-thaw; whether the eave-drops fall
Heard only in the trances of the blast,

Or if the secret ministry of frost
Shall hang them up in silent icicles,
Quietly shining to the quiet Moon.

BILLY COLLINS   *(b. 1952)*

Today I pass the time reading
a favorite haiku,
saying the few words over and over.

It feels like eating
the same small, perfect grape
again and again.

I walk through the house reciting it
and leave its letters falling
through the air of every room.

I stand by the big silence of the piano and say it.
I say it in front of a painting of the sea.
I tap out its rhythm on an empty shelf.

I listen to myself saying it,
then I say it without listening,
then I hear it without saying it.

And when the dog looks up at me,
I kneel down on the floor
and whisper it into each of his long white ears.

It's the one about the one-ton
temple bell
with the moth sleeping on its surface,

and every time I say it, I feel the excruciating
pressure of the moth
on the surface of the iron bell.

When I say it at the window,
the bell is the world
and I am the moth resting there.

When I say it into the mirror,
I am the heavy bell
and the moth is life with its papery wings.

And later, when I say it to you in the dark,
you are the bell,
and I am the tongue of the bell, ringing you,

and the moth has flown
from its line
and moves like a hinge in the air above our bed.

JAMES DICKEY   *(1923–1997)*

Here they are. The soft eyes open.
If they have lived in a wood
It is a wood.
If they have lived on plains
It is grass rolling
Under their feet forever.

Having no souls, they have come,
Anyway, beyond their knowing.
Their instincts wholly bloom
And they rise.
The soft eyes open.

To match them, the landscape flowers,
Outdoing, desperately
Outdoing what is required:
The richest wood,
The deepest field.

For some of these,
It could not be the place
It is, without blood.
These hunt, as they have done,
But with claws and teeth grown perfect,

More deadly than they can believe.
They stalk more silently,
And crouch on the limbs of trees,
And their descent
Upon the bright backs of their prey

May take years
In a sovereign floating of joy.

And those that are hunted
Know this as their life,
Their reward: to walk

Under such trees in full knowledge
Of what is in glory above them,
And to feel no fear,
But acceptance, compliance.
Fulfilling themselves without pain

At the cycle's center,
They tremble, they walk
Under the tree,
They fall, they are torn,
They rise, they walk again.

EMILY DICKINSON   *(1830–1886)*

I taste a liquor never brewed—
From Tankards scooped in Pearl—
Not all the Vats upon the Rhine
Yield such an Alcohol!

Inebriate of Air—am I—
And Debauchee of Dew—
Reeling—thro endless summer days—
From inns of Molten Blue—

When "Landlords" turn the drunken Bee
Out of the Foxglove's door—
When Butterflies—renounce their "drams"—
I shall but drink the more!

Till Seraphs swing their snowy Hats—
And Saints—to windows run—
To see the little Tippler
Leaning against the—Sun—

#1463

EMILY DICKINSON   (1830–1886)

A Route of Evanescence
With a revolving Wheel—
A Resonance of Emerald—
A Rush of Cochineal—
And every Blossom on the Bush
Adjusts its tumbled Head—
The mail from Tunis, probably,
An easy Morning's Ride—

[Note: This is a riddle poem; for the answer, see biographical notes.]

EMILY DICKINSON   *(1830–1886)*

I'll tell you how the Sun rose—
A Ribbon at a time—
The Steeples swam in Amethyst—
The news, like Squirrels, ran—
The Hills untied their Bonnets—
The Bobolinks—begun—
Then I said softly to myself—
"That must have been the Sun"!
But how he set—I knew not—
There seemed a purple stile*
That little Yellow boys and girls
Were climbing all the while—
Till when they reached the other side,
A Dominie† in Gray—
Put gently up the evening Bars—
And led the flock away—

*steps arranged to allow one person at a time over or through a fence
†schoolmaster

EMILY DICKINSON   (1830–1886)

As if I asked a common Alms,
And in my wondering hand
A Stranger pressed a Kingdom,
And I, bewildered, stand—
As if I asked the Orient
Had it for me a Morn—
And it should lift its purple Dikes,
And shatter me with Dawn!

PEAR TREE

H.D. (HILDA DOOLITTLE)   *(1884–1961)*

Silver dust
lifted from the earth,
higher than my arms reach,
you have mounted,
O silver,
higher than my arms reach
you front us with great mass;

no flower ever opened
so staunch a white leaf,
no flower ever parted silver
from such rare silver;
O white pear,
your flower-tufts
thick on the branch
bring summer and ripe fruits
in their purple hearts.

DUST OF SNOW

ROBERT FROST   *(1874–1963)*

The way a crow
Shook down on me
The dust of snow
From a hemlock tree

Has given my heart
A change of mood
And saved some part
Of a day I had rued.

BLUE-BUTTERFLY DAY

ROBERT FROST   *(1874–1963)*

It is a blue-butterfly day here in spring,
And with these sky-flakes down in flurry on flurry
There is more unmixed color on the wing
Than flowers will show for days unless they hurry.

But these are flowers that fly and all but sing:
And now from having ridden out desire
They lie closed over in the wind and cling
Where wheels have freshly sliced the April mire.

STOPPING BY WOODS ON A SNOWY EVENING

ROBERT FROST   *(1874–1963)*

Whose woods these are I think I know
His house is in the village, though;
He will not see me stopping here
To watch his woods fill up with snow.

My little horse must think it queer
To stop without a farmhouse near
Between the woods and frozen lake
The darkest evening of the year.

He gives his harness bells a shake
To ask if there is some mistake.
The only other sound's the sweep
Of easy wind and downy flake.

The woods are lovely, dark, and deep,
But I have promises to keep,
And miles to go before I sleep,
And miles to go before I sleep.

MARIA MAZZIOTTI GILLAN   (b. 1943)

We are standing in a backyard.
Part of a porch is visible, a lattice
heavy with roses, a small tree.
Beyond the bushes in the background,
a woman with her hand on her hip
stares at us.

My father is young. He squints
into the sun. He wears a white shirt,
a flowered tie, a pair of gabardine pants
and dress shoes. His hair is thick
and crew cut. My mother wears high-heeled
black shoes with a strap across the ankle
and nylons and a black dress
printed with large flowers,
her hair, bobbed and neat.
Her arm, bent at the elbow,
looks strong and firm.
I cannot see her expression clearly,
but I think she is smiling.
Her hand is on my sister Laura's arm,
Laura stands between them.
She is thirteen, her skin clear and beautiful.

Alex and I share a small stool
in front of the three grouped
behind us, my long hair drawn back
in a straight line. I sit
behind him. He is about seven,
slim and dressed up in imitation

of my father, except Alex wears
a bow tie. His knees look sharp
and boney through his pants,
his hands clasped together
between his knees.

Even in the standard family picture,
we do not look American.

I think of my mother's preparations:
The rough feel of the washcloth
and Lifebuoy soap against my face,
the stiff, starched feel of my blouse,
the streets of Paterson, old and cracked,
the houses leaning together
like crooked teeth, the yards
that grow larger as we climb the hill,
the immigrant gardens.

We walk back home
in early evening, after the grown-ups
have espresso and anisette and
we, small jelly glasses of juice.
My brother's hand in mine, I pretend
to be grown up. Dreams
cluster around my head
like a halo, while crickets
fill the summer evening
with their shining web of song.

MARIA MAZZIOTTI GILLAN   (b. 1943)

I
On my neighbor's roof, plastic butterflies
freeze in rigid postures. Rubber ducks waddle
into trimmed evergreens; plaster cats climb
siding toward peaked roofs.

Once, in a vacant Paterson lot, I caught
a butterfly; the lot seemed huge. Daisies
grew there and marigolds and red berries
which stained our fingers. We had crepe paper
whirlers in varied colors; we spun and spun.
The whirlers were an army of insects
buzzing, till tall grass and flowers blurred.

The butterfly in my hand beat its wings
in terror. My hand stained gold.
When I let it escape it flew away fast,
and then, forgetting, it dipped and swirled
so gracefully I almost stopped breathing.

II
By 9 each morning, Oak Place with its neat box
houses lies still and empty. Children have vanished
into yellow camp buses, parents departed in separate cars.

The street settles into somnolence. Its lines
and angles imprison handkerchief lawns
until even the old oaks no longer seem at home.
In my yesterdays I dreamed myself out of the old city,
imagining a world just like this one,
away from strewn garbage and houses stacked close as teeth.

Today I mourn tomatoes ripening in our immigrant gardens,
the pattern of sun on walls of old brick mills,
a time when each day opened like a morning glory.
Some days when I look at my hand, I imagine
it is still stained gold.

SUNFLOWER SUTRA

ALLEN GINSBERG   (1926–1997)

I walked on the banks of the tincan banana dock and sat
   down under the huge shade of a Southern Pacific
   locomotive to look at the sunset over the box house hills
   and cry.
Jack Kerouac sat beside me on a busted rusty iron pole,
   companion, we thought the same thoughts of the soul,
   bleak and blue and sad-eyed, surrounded by the gnarled
   steel roots of trees of machinery.
The oily water on the river mirrored the red sky, sun sank on
   top of final Frisco peaks, no fish in that stream, no hermit
   in those mounts, just ourselves rheumy-eyed and
   hungover like old bums on the riverbank, tired and wily.
Look at the Sunflower, he said, there was a dead gray shadow
   against the sky, big as a man, sitting dry on top of a pile
   of ancient sawdust—
—I rushed up enchanted—it was my first sunflower,
   memories of Blake—my visions—Harlem
and Hells of the Eastern rivers, bridges clanking Joes Greasy
   Sandwiches, dead baby carriages, black treadless tires
   forgotten and unretreaded, the poem of the riverbank,
   condoms & pots, steel knives, nothing stainless, only
   the dank muck and the razor sharp artifacts passing into
   the past—
and the gray Sunflower poised against the sunset, crackly
   bleak and dusty with the smut and smog and smoke of
   olden locomotives in its eye—
corolla of bleary spikes pushed down and broken like a
   battered crown, seeds fallen out of its face, soon-to-be-
   toothless mouth of sunny air, sunrays obliterated on its
   hairy head like a dried wire spiderweb,
leaves stuck out like arms out of the stem, gestures from the

sawdust root, broke pieces of plaster fallen out of the
black twigs, a dead fly in its ear,
Unholy battered old thing you were, my sunflower O my
soul, I loved you then!
The grime was no man's grime but death and human
locomotives,
all that dress of dust, that veil of darkened railroad skin, that
smog of cheek, that eyelid of black mis'ry, that sooty hand
or phallus or protuberance of artificial worse-than-dirt—
industrial—modern—all that civilization spotting your
crazy golden crown—
and those blear thoughts of death and dusty loveless eyes
and ends and withered roots below, in the home-pile of
sand and sawdust, rubber dollar bills, skin of machinery,
the guts and innards of the weeping coughing car, the
empty lonely tincans with their rusty tongues alack, what
more could I name, the smoked ashes of some cock cigar,
the cunts of wheelbarrows and the milky breasts of cars,
wornout asses out of chairs & sphincters of dynamos—
all these
entangled in your mummied roots—and you there standing
before me in the sunset, all your glory in your form!
A perfect beauty of a sunflower! a perfect excellent lovely
sunflower existence! a sweet natural eye to the new hip
moon, woke up alive and excited grasping in the sunset
shadow sunrise golden monthly breeze!
How many flies buzzed round you innocent of your grime,
while you cursed the heavens of the railroad and your
flower soul?
Poor dead flower? when did you forget you were a flower?
when did you look at your skin and decide you were an
impotent dirty old locomotive? the ghost of a locomotive?
the specter and shade of a once powerful mad American
locomotive?

You were never no locomotive, Sunflower, you were a
    sunflower!
And you Locomotive, you are a locomotive, forget me not!
So I grabbed up the skeleton thick sunflower and stuck it at
    my side like a scepter,
and deliver my sermon to my soul, and Jack's soul too, and
    anyone who'll listen,
—We're not our skin of grime, we're not our dread bleak
    dusty imageless locomotive, we're all beautiful golden
    sunflowers inside, we're blessed by our own seed & golden
    hairy naked accomplishment-bodies growing into mad
    black formal sunflowers in the sunset, spied on by our
    eyes under the shadow of the mad locomotive riverbank
    sunset Frisco hilly tincan evening sitdown vision.

A POEM ENDING IN THE PREPOSITION "WITH"

MICHAEL S. GLASER   *(b. 1943)*

"You can fail love, but love will never fail you."

. . . an idea so luminous,
so . . . so . . . amazing

that most of us
have to make up conditions:

Thus, love comes free,
but not for you or me.

we have to deserve it,
we have to be worthy of it

and thus we live for the if of ever
wondering always whether

we have failed again
or have somehow earned

what was always there to begin
with.

THE BLACK FINGER

ANGELINA WELD GRIMKÉ   *(1880–1958)*

I have just seen a beautiful thing
          Slim and still,
Against a gold, gold sky,
          A straight cypress,
          Sensitive
          Exquisite,
A black finger
Pointing upwards.
Why, beautiful, still finger are you black?
And why are you pointing upwards?

THOSE WINTER SUNDAYS

ROBERT HAYDEN   *(1913–1980)*

Sundays too my father got up early
and put his clothes on in the blueblack cold,
then with cracked hands that ached
from labor in the weekday weather made
banked fires blaze. No one ever thanked him.

I'd wake and hear the cold splintering, breaking.
When the rooms were warm, he'd call,
and slowly I would rise and dress,
fearing the chronic angers of that house,

Speaking indifferently to him,
who had driven out the cold
and polished my good shoes as well.
What did I know, what did I know
of love's austere and lonely offices?

INVICTUS

WILLIAM ERNEST HENLEY   *(1849–1903)*

Out of the night that covers me,
Black as the Pit from pole to pole,
I thank whatever gods may be
For my unconquerable soul.

In the fell clutch of circumstance
I have not winced nor cried aloud.
Under the bludgeonings of chance
My head is bloody, but unbowed.

Beyond this place of wrath and tears
Looms but the horror of the shade,
And yet the menace of the years
Finds and shall find me unafraid.

It matters not how strait the gate,
How charged with punishments the scroll,
I am the master of my fate;
I am the captain of my soul.

GEORGE HERBERT   *(1593–1633)*

Sweet day, so cool, so calm, so bright,
   The bridal of the earth and sky:
The dew shall weep thy fall tonight;
     For thou must die.

Sweet rose, whose hue, angry and brave,
   Bids the rash gazer wipe his eye:
Thy root is ever in its grave,
     And thou must die.

Sweet spring, full of sweet days and roses,
   A box where sweets compacted lie;
My music shows ye have your closes,
     And all must die.

Only a sweet and virtuous soul,
   Like seasoned timber, never gives;
But though the whole world turn to coal,
     Then chiefly lives.

MARIE HOWE   *(b. 1950)*

Johnny, the kitchen sink has been clogged for days, some
    utensil probably fell down there.
And the Drano won't work but smells dangerous, and the
    crusty dishes have piled up

waiting for the plumber I still haven't called. This is the
    everyday we spoke of.
It's winter again: the sky's a deep headstrong blue, and the
    sunlight pours through

the open living room windows because the heat's on too
    high in here, and I can't turn it off.
For weeks now, driving, or dropping a bag of groceries in the
    street, the bag breaking,

I've been thinking: This is what the living do. And yesterday,
    hurrying along those
wobbly bricks in the Cambridge sidewalk, spilling my coffee
    down my wrist and sleeve,

I thought it again, and again later, when buying a hairbrush:
    This is it.
Parking. Slamming the car door shut in the cold. What you
    called *that yearning*.

What you finally gave up. We want the spring to come and
    the winter to pass. We want
whoever to call or not call, a letter, a kiss—we want more
    and more and then more of it.

But there are moments, walking, when I catch a glimpse of
    myself in the window glass,
say, the window of the corner video store, and I'm gripped
    by a cherishing so deep

for my own blowing hair, chapped face, and unbuttoned
   coat that I'm speechless:
I am living, I remember you.

LANGSTON HUGHES   *(1902–1967)*

I went down to the river,
I set down on the bank.
I tried to think but couldn't,
So I jumped in and sank.

I came up once and hollered!
I came up twice and cried!
If that water hadn't a-been so cold
I might've sunk and died.

    But it was
    Cold in that water!
    It was cold!

I took the elevator
Sixteen floors above the ground.
I thought about my baby
And thought I would jump down.

I stood there and I hollered!
I stood there and I cried!
If it hadn't a-been so high
I might've jumped and died.

    But it was
    High up there!
    It was high!

So since I'm still here livin',
I guess I will live on.
I could've died for love—
But for livin' I was born.

Though you may hear me holler,
And you may see me cry—
I'll be dogged, sweet baby,
If you gonna see me die.

Life is fine!
Fine as wine!
Life is fine!

RONDEAU

LEIGH HUNT   *(1784–1859)*

Jenny kissed me when we met,
  Jumping from the chair she sat in;
Time, you thief, who love to get
  Sweets into your list, put that in:
Say I'm weary, say I'm sad,
  Say that health and wealth have missed me,
Say I'm growing old, but add,
  Jenny kissed me.

READING AT NIGHT

DAVID IGNATOW   *(1914–1997)*

What have I learned that can keep me
from the simple fact of my dying?
None of the ideas I read stay
with me for long, I find the dark
closed in about me as I close
the book and I hurry to open it
again to let its light shine
on my face.

HAIKU

ISSA   *(1763–1827)*

Climb Mount Fuji,
O snail,
   but slowly, slowly.

Translated from the Japanese by Robert Hass

LOOK

ROLF JACOBSEN   *(1907–1994)*

The moon thumbs through the night's book.
Finds a lake where nothing is printed.
Draws a straight line. That's all
it can. That's enough.
Thick line. Straight toward you.
—Look.

Translated from the Norwegian by Olav Grinde

THE RED DRESS

VICKIE KARP   *(b. 1953)*

Some autumn leaves create a space in the shape of a
    red dress.
Faceless, heartless, cool
Where the eyes would be, it makes a rather artless citizen

Floating sulkily above a pedestal of maples, an inadvertent
    fund of spirits
For some other planet whose weary inhabitants can't
    reach Earth.

There is a tiny body that lives its entire life inside our mind,
The ultimate hermit, the chaste lover who stays
For the sake of something that happened long ago,
    something

We originally thought little about that has had
    consequences,
Like a good Greek tragedy.

"That is the dress I want to wear when I die," I tell the
    hermit.
"When I am no longer the terrified audience, the translator
    between us,
When you and I, after years of betrayals, switch places."

TO AUTUMN

JOHN KEATS   (1795–1821)

Season of mists and mellow fruitfulness,
    Close bosom-friend of the maturing sun;
Conspiring with him how to load and bless
    With fruit the vines that round the thatch-eaves run;
To bend with apples the mossed cottage-trees,
    And fill all fruit with ripeness to the core;
        To swell the gourd, and plump the hazel shells
    With a sweet kernel; to set budding more,
And still more, later flowers for the bees,
Until they think warm days will never cease,
        For Summer has o'er-brimmed their clammy cells.

Who hath not seen thee oft amid thy store?
    Sometimes whoever seeks abroad may find
Thee sitting careless on a granary floor,
    Thy hair soft-lifted by the winnowing wind;
Or on a half-reaped furrow sound asleep,
    Drowsed with the fume of poppies, while thy hook
        Spares the next swath and all its twinéd flowers:
And sometimes like a gleaner thou dost keep
    Steady thy laden head across a brook;
    Or by a cider-press, with patient look,
        Thou watchest the last oozings hours by hours.

Where are the songs of Spring? Aye, where are they?
    Think not of them, thou hast thy music too—
While barréd clouds bloom the soft-dying day,
    And touch the stubble-plains with rosy hue;
Then in a wailful choir the small gnats mourn
    Among the river sallows, borne aloft
        Or sinking as the light wind lives or dies;

And full-grown lambs loud bleat from hilly bourn;*
    Hedge crickets sing; and now with treble soft
    The redbreast whistles from a garden-croft;
        And gathering swallows twitter in the skies.

*field

PEONIES AT DUSK

JANE KENYON   (1947–1995)

White peonies blooming along the porch
send out light
while the rest of the yard grows dim.

Outrageous flowers as big as human
heads! They're staggered
by their own luxuriance: I had
to prop them up with stakes and twine.

The moist air intensifies their scent,
and the moon moves around the barn
to find out what it's coming from.

In the darkening June evening
I draw a blossom near, and bending close
search it as a woman searches
a loved one's face.

JANE KENYON   *(1947–1995)*

Let the light of late afternoon
shine through chinks in the barn, moving
up the bales as the sun moves down.

Let the cricket take up chafing
as a woman takes up her needles
and her yarn. Let evening come.

Let dew collect on the hoe abandoned
in long grass. Let the stars appear
and the moon disclose her silver horn.

Let the fox go back to its sandy den.
Let the wind die down. Let the shed
go black inside. Let evening come.

To the bottle in the ditch, to the scoop
in the oats, to air in the lung
let evening come.

Let it come, as it will, and don't
be afraid. God does not leave us
comfortless, so let evening come.

AWAKE!

OMAR KHAYYÁM   *(d. 1123)*

Awake! For Morning in the Bowl of Night
Has flung the Stone that puts the Stars to Flight:
And Lo! The Hunter of the East has Caught
The Sultan's Turret in a Noose of Light.

From the English version of the Rubáiyát of Omar Khayyám *translated by Edward FitzGerald*

DAS LANZILLOTTI   *(b. 1950)*

On days like this . . .
Before the dawn ever happens
when the sky is still dark
and the morning star bright. It is
on days like this . . .
When the last of the night spills
    into the ravine.
When my mind is filled with the
thoughts of smooth stones.
It is on days like this . . .
When the garden is damp
And the wind
still trapped
    inside my ear.
And I find the same pebble twice
    when my pocket is full
it is on days like this . . .
It is on days exactly like this . . .

BEI HENNEF*

D. H. LAWRENCE   (1885–1930)

The little river twittering in the twilight,
The wan, wandering look of the pale sky,
   This is almost bliss.

And everything shut up and gone to sleep,
All the troubles and anxieties and pain
   Gone under the twilight.

Only the twilight now, and the soft "Sh!" of the river
   That will last for ever.

And at last I know my love for you is here;
I can see it all, it is whole like the twilight
It is large, so large, I could not see it before,
Because of the little lights and flickers and interruptions,
   Troubles, anxieties and pains.

You are the call and I am the answer,
You are the wish, and I the fulfillment,
You are the night, and I the day.
   What else? It is perfect enough.
   It is perfectly complete,
   You and I,
   What more—?

Strange, how we suffer in spite of this!

*Hennef is a place Lawrence visited in Germany.

SONG OF A MAN WHO HAS COME THROUGH

D. H. LAWRENCE   *(1885–1930)*

Not I, not I, but the wind that blows through me!
A fine wind is blowing the new direction of Time.
If only I let it bear me, carry me, if only it carry me!
If only I am sensitive, subtle, oh, delicate, a winged gift!
If only, most lovely of all, I yield myself and am borrowed
By the fine, fine wind that takes its course through the chaos of
    The world
Like a fine, an exquisite chisel, a wedge-blade inserted;
If only I am keen and hard like the sheer tip of a wedge
Driven by invisible blows,
The rock will split, we shall come at the wonder, we shall
    find the Hesperides.*

Oh, for the wonder that bubbles into my soul,
I would be a good fountain, a good well-head,
Would blur no whisper, spoil no expression.

What is the knocking?
What is the knocking at the door in the night?
It is somebody wants to do us harm.
No, no, it is the three strange angels.
Admit them, admit them.

---

*In Greek myth, Hesperides is the name of the nymphs who guarded golden apples and
the garden in which they lived.

RECUERDO

EDNA ST. VINCENT MILLAY   *(1892–1950)*

We were very tired, we were very merry—
We had gone back and forth all night on the ferry.
It was bare and bright, and smelled like a stable—
But we looked into a fire, we leaned across a table,
We lay on a hill-top underneath the moon;
And the whistles kept blowing, and the dawn came soon.

We were very tired, we were very merry—
We had gone back and forth all night on the ferry;
And you ate an apple, and I ate a pear,
From a dozen of each we had bought somewhere;
And the sky went wan, and the wind came cold,
And the sun rose dripping, a bucketful of gold.

We were very tired, we were very merry,
We had gone back and forth all night on the ferry.
We hailed, "Good morrow, mother!" to a
    shawl-covered head
And bought a morning paper, which neither of us read;
And she wept, "God bless you!" for the apples and pears,
And we gave her all our money but our subway fares.

FIRST FIG

EDNA ST. VINCENT MILLAY   *(1892–1950)*

My candle burns at both ends;
    It will not last the night;
But ah, my foes, and oh, my friends—
    It gives a lovely light!

SECOND FIG

Safe upon the solid rock the ugly houses stand:
Come and see my shining palace built upon the sand!

HAIKU

ARAKIDA MORITAKE   *(1473–1549)*

When I think of it
As my snow, how light it feels
On my bamboo hat.

REVENGE

AMADO NERVO   *(1870–1919)*

There are those who will throw a rock at my roof, and then
hypocritically hide the quick hands
that ruined me . . .
I have no rocks, for
in my garden there are only fragrant arbors
of fresh roses, and yet my idiosyncrasy is—
I too hide my hand after throwing the roses.

Translated from the Spanish by Alvin Delgado and Liz Rosenberg

ECSTASY

AMADO NERVO   *(1870–1919)*

Each tender rose born yesterday
each dawn that mends between blushes
loses my soul in ecstasy . . .
My eyes never tire of gazing
at the perpetual miracle of life!

Years ago, I contemplated the stars
in the diaphanous Spanish nights
and found them more beautiful each time.
For years, by the sea, alone,
I heard the waves complain,
and still I am stunned by the marvel of those waves!

Each time I find Nature
more supernatural, more pure and saintly.
For me—everything everywhere is beauty;
and I am as fully enchanted by
the mouth of the mother praying,
the mouth of the child singing.

  I passionately want to be immortal
because it is marvellous, the panorama
of this immense creation;
because every brilliant star claims me,
telling me as it shines, "Here, too, we think,
here, too, we struggle, here we love!"

Translated from the Spanish by Alvin Delgado and Liz Rosenberg

HAVING A COKE WITH YOU

FRANK O'HARA   (1926–1966)

is even more fun than going to San Sebastian, Irún,
    Hendaye, Biarritz, Bayonne
or being sick to my stomach on the Travesera de Gracia in
    Barcelona
partly because in your orange shirt you look like a better
    happier St. Sebastian
partly because of my love for you, partly because of your
    love for yoghurt
partly because of the fluorescent orange tulips around the
    birches
partly because of the secrecy our smiles take on before
    people and statuary
it is hard to believe when I'm with you that there can be
    anything as still
as solemn as unpleasantly definitive as statuary when right in
    front of it
in the warm New York 4 o'clock light we are drifting back
    and forth
between each other like a tree breathing through its
    spectacles

and the portrait show seems to have no faces in it at all,
    just paint
you suddenly wonder why in the world anyone ever
    did them
                                        I look
at you and I would rather look at you than all the portraits
    in the world
except possibly for the *Polish Rider* occasionally and anyway
    it's in the Frick

which thank heavens you haven't gone to yet so we can go
together the first time
and the fact that you move so beautifully more or less takes
care of Futurism
just as at home I never think of the *Nude Descending a
Staircase* or
at a rehearsal a single drawing of Leonardo or Michelangelo
that used to wow me
and what good does all the research of the Impressionists
do them
when they never got the right person to stand near the tree
when the sun sank
or for that matter Marino Marini when he didn't pick the
rider as carefully
as the horse
                it seems they were all cheated of some marvellous
experience
which is not going to go wasted on me which is why I'm
telling you about it

THE SUMMER DAY

MARY OLIVER   *(b. 1935)*

Who made the world?
Who made the swan, and the black bear?
Who made the grasshopper?
This grasshopper, I mean—
the one who has flung herself out of the grass,
the one who is eating sugar out of my hand,
who is moving her jaws back and forth instead of up
    and down—
who is gazing around with her enormous and
    complicated eyes.
Now she lifts her pale forearms and thoroughly washes
    her face.
Now she snaps her wings open, and floats away.
I don't know exactly what a prayer is.
I do know how to pay attention, how to fall down
into the grass, how to kneel down in the grass,
how to be idle and blessed, how to stroll through the fields,
which is what I have been doing all day.
Tell me, what else should I have done?
Doesn't everything die at last, and too soon?
Tell me, what is it you plan to do
with your one wild and precious life?

PSALMIST   *(attributed to King David, c. 1000 B.C.E.)*

The Lord is my shepherd; I shall not want.
He maketh me to lie down in green pastures: he leadeth me
    beside the still waters.
He restoreth my soul: he leadeth me in the paths of
    righteousness for his name's sake.
Yea, though I walk through the valley of the shadow of
    death, I will fear no evil: for thou art with me; thy rod
    and thy staff they comfort me.
Thou preparest a table before me in the presence of mine
    enemies: thou anointest my head with oil; my cup
    runneth over.
Surely goodness and mercy shall follow me all the days of
    my life: and I will dwell in the house of the Lord for ever.

AFTER I HAD WORKED ALL DAY

CHARLES REZNIKOFF   *(1894–1976)*

After I had worked all day at what I earn my living,
I was tired. Now my own work has lost another day,
I thought, but began slowly,
and slowly my strength came back to me.
Surely, the tide comes in twice a day.

I WAS WEARING A BELT BUCKLE

CHARLES REZNIKOFF   *(1894–1976)*

I was wearing a belt buckle
with the initial of my family name on it
in a cheap design. A friend noticed it
and I said apologetically:
"This was my father's. He had no taste."
"Perhaps," my friend answered gently,
"he wore it because it was a gift."

AUTUMN

RAINER MARIA RILKE   *(1875–1926)*

The leaves are falling, falling as if from far up,
as if orchards were dying high in space.
Each leaf falls as if it were motioning "no."

And tonight the heavy earth is falling
away from all the other stars in the loneliness.

We're all falling. This hand here is falling.
And look at the other one . . . It's in them all.

And yet there is Someone, whose hands
infinitely calm, hold up all this falling.

Translated from the German by Robert Bly

THE MAN WATCHING

RAINER MARIA RILKE   *(1875–1926)*

I can tell by the way the trees beat, after
so many dull days, on my worried windowpanes
that a storm is coming,
and I hear the far-off fields say things
I can't bear without a friend,
I can't love without a sister.

The storm, the shifter of shapes, drives on
across the woods and across time,
and the world looks as if it had no age:
the landscape, like a line in the psalm book,
is seriousness and weight and eternity.

What we fight is so small!
What struggles with us is so great!
If only we would let ourselves be dominated
as things do by some immense storm,
we would become strong too, and not need names.

When we win it's with small things,
and the triumph itself makes us small.
What is extraordinary and eternal
does not *want* to be bent by us.
I mean the Angel who appeared
to the wrestlers of the Old Testament:
when the wrestlers' sinews
grew long like metal strings,
he felt them under his fingers
like chords of deep music.

Whoever was beaten by this Angel
(who often simply declined the fight)
went away proud and strengthened

and great from that harsh hand,
that kneaded him as if to change his shape.
Winning does not tempt that one.
This is how he grows: by being defeated, decisively,
by constantly greater beings.

Translated from the German by Robert Bly

GOLD

LIZ ROSENBERG   (b. 1956)

I stand shaking inside my panic-skin
at the foot of my son's bed, watching him
shake off the last rags of his morning dreams.
He smiles, opens his eyes, frowns his Beethoven frown,
then pats the narrow ledge of bed beside him
and humbly I crawl in. Three pills a half an hour ago
to make me sane, but still I shiver
and he begins to sing:
"If I had words to make a day for you,
I'd sing a morning golden and true."
He kisses me, his rounded cheek like risen bread.
This morning, after hours of nightmares
I had this dream: a boy rode on bicycle,
and led my son and me to a hill of high, gold grass.
At the foot of it lay a cove of water, gentle and blue.
I said, "How did this water get here? Where are we?"
and the boy answered, "It's always been here."
Just then, a flock of waterbirds rose up and flew
and when I turned around, I saw a line
of children ready to run down.
My own boy sings to me in his golden treble
as if he were a character in my dream. But he is real,
and the dream—also real. In dreams the soul confronts
and then converses with itself; in shades of blue
and violet and green and teal, a scarf hangs in the closet
on the grayest day, lighting the room.
Just so, in most exquisite happiness
we find ourselves at the verge of tears.
Gloom, dream, and singing boy
in the high gold grass that has always been here.

LIZ ROSENBERG   *(b. 1956)*

I want to live among the big, bell-like and moving things
with purple beach pea flowers opening
and closing, day into night the beam
casting across the foam.

Summer stars and Roman candles have drowned
themselves hissing down against the black
and gold-lit sea, washing with sailors' caps
at the last thin curve of the Cape, the Light
a pulse of safety when a child
awakens, feels car headlights rake
ceiling and bed, the emptiness of space,

and crosses to the window and looks out.
Then daybreak of the lighthouse swings,
goes steadily across the wall—
a blinking owl at the windowpane,
dragging the mirrored blackness out,
bringing a shining seaweed twig or flowering wave to shore.

I want to live like that,
to be a great and watchful eye
that sends all its light out and takes nothing back.

HURT NO LIVING THING

CHRISTINA ROSSETTI   *(1836–1894)*

Hurt no living thing:
   Ladybird, nor butterfly,
Nor moth with dusty wing,
   Nor cricket chirping cheerily,
Nor grasshopper so light of leap,
   Nor dancing gnat, nor beetle fat,
Nor harmless worms that creep.

RUMI   *(1207–1273)*

When I am with you, we stay up all night.
When you're not here, I can't go to sleep.

Praise God for these two insomnias!
And the difference between them.

Translated from the Persian by Coleman Barks

RUMI   *(1207–1273)*

Come to the orchard in Spring.
There is light and wine, and sweethearts in the pomegranate
    flowers.
If you do not come, these do not matter.
If you do come, these do not matter.

Translated from the Persian by Coleman Barks

RUMI   *(1207–1273)*

Today, like every other day, we wake up empty
and frightened. Don't open the door to the study
and begin reading. Take down a musical instrument.

Let the beauty we love be what we do.
There are hundreds of ways to kneel and kiss the ground.

Translated from the Persian by Coleman Barks

WISHING WELL

KATE SCHMITT *(b. 1973)*

The mesh of the blanket tangles
and lumps of comforter
two-toned flannel and bedspread
twist and slip.

I haven't slept in a week
so I wear my brown hooded
sweatshirt with the hoodstrings
pulled tightly around my face.

I picture a wishing well
with edges of greening minerals
and coins dull with old water.
I throw my wish in a copper arc.

After I've thrown it I lie
unconcerned. These things take time.

KATE SCHMITT   *(b. 1973)*

I often think of him looking sideways
at me and the painting he did for me
of the little girl who may look alone
but really isn't at all.
We listened to the War of the Worlds
and I fell asleep during the broadcast,
fingers fluttering against the pillowcase.

I think of the idea of a heart,
the idea that the constant rocking
inside us that keeps us alive
could be responsible for a feeling.
I think of the pink and red hearts cut
up and pasted onto construction paper.
What could these possibly have to say
to the muscle in the chest?

There is something else, too.
There is desire and what does it
have to do with anything? I remember
reading that eagles join together in flight,
but in love they can no longer fly
so they plummet like siamese twins
toward the trees, no thought for ground.

I think of these eagles picking up speed
and I want this feeling—
To be so willing to fall!

HENRY M. SEIDEN   (b. 1940)

I'm stopped at a light in Flushing behind a truck
which says *General Coatings*. I think,
joke: he must have been a hero in the War . . .
then idling in the blue of the exhaust
I think of the layers we all have on us, generally:
like experience over innocence, and I think,
Now there's a business this world needs—
they come to your house and you get coated,
sprayed with something glowing, something
impervious, which shows you off to best advantage.
A youthful green over sick & tired. Or a rosiness
over sad & cynical. Or a coating of laughter.
Of laughing over your crying.
Not to expect that the crying goes away.
No, you can see it as if under glass.
But the crying-under deepens the joke.
Everybody knows that. Just looking at yourself
you see it.

TO JANE: THE KEEN STARS WERE TWINKLING

PERCY BYSSHE SHELLEY   *(1792–1822)*

1

The keen stars were twinkling,
And the fair moon was rising among them,
    Dear Jane!
    The guitar was tinkling,
But the notes were not sweet till you sung them
    Again.

2

As the moon's soft splendor
O'er the faint cold starlight of Heaven
    Is thrown,
    So your voice most tender
To the strings without soul had then given
    Its own.

3

The stars will awaken,
Though the moon sleep a full hour later,
    Tonight;
    No leaf will be shaken
Whilst the dews of your melody scatter
    Delight.

4

Though the sound overpowers,
Sing again, with your dear voice revealing
    A tone
    Of some world far from ours,
Where music and moonlight and feeling
    Are one.

PERCY BYSSHE SHELLEY   *(1792–1822)*

Make me thy lyre, even as the forest is:
What if my leaves are falling like its own!
The tumult of thy mighty harmonies

Will take from both a deep, autumnal tone,
Sweet though in sadness. Be thou, Spirit fierce,
My spirit! Be thou me, impetuous one!

Drive my dead thoughts over the universe
Like withered leaves to quicken a new birth!
And, by the incantation of this verse,

Scatter, as from an unextinguished hearth
Ashes and sparks, my words among mankind!
Be through my lips to unawakened earth

The trumpet of a prophecy! O Wind,
If Winter comes, can Spring be far behind?

CHRISTOPHER SMART   (1722–1771)

For I will consider my Cat Jeoffry.

For he is the servant of the Living God, duly and daily
serving him.

For at the first glance of the glory of God in the East he
worships in his way.

For is this done by wreathing his body seven times round
with elegant quickness.

For then he leaps up to catch the musk, which is the blessing
of God upon his prayer.

For he rolls upon prank to work it in.

For having done duty and received blessing he begins to
consider himself.

For this he performs in ten degrees.

For first he looks upon his forepaws to see if they are clean.

For secondly he kicks up behind to clear away there.

For thirdly he works it upon stretch with the forepaws
extended.

For fourthly he sharpens his paws by wood.

For fifthly he washes himself.

For sixthly he rolls upon wash.

For seventhly he fleas himself, that he may not be
interrupted upon the beat.

For eighthly he rubs himself against a post.

For ninthly he looks up for his instructions.

For tenthly he goes in quest of food.

For having considered God and himself he will consider his
neighbor.

For if he meets another cat he will kiss her in kindness.

For when he takes his prey he plays with it to give it a
chance.

For one mouse in seven escapes by his dallying.

For when his day's work is done his business more properly
  begins.
For he keeps the Lord's watch in the night against the
  adversary.
For he counteracts the powers of darkness by his electrical
  skin and glaring eyes.
For he counteracts the Devil, who is death, by brisking
  about the life.
For in his morning orisons he loves the sun and the sun
  loves him.
For he is of the tribe of Tiger.
For the Cherub Cat is a term of the Angel Tiger.
For he has the subtlety and hissing of a serpent, which in
  goodness he suppresses.
For he will not do destruction if he is well-fed, neither will
  he spit without provocation.
For he purrs in thankfulness when God tells him he's a
  good Cat.
For he is an instrument for the children to learn
  benevolence upon.
For every house is incomplete without him, and a blessing is
  lacking in the spirit.
For the Lord commanded Moses concerning the cats at the
  departure of the Children of Israel from Egypt.
For every family had one cat at least in the bag.
For the English Cats are the best in Europe.
For he is the cleanest in the use of his forepaws of any
  quadruped.
For the dexterity of his defense is an instance of the love of
  God to him exceedingly.
For he is the quickest to his mark of any creature.
For he is tenacious of his point.
For he is a mixture of gravity and waggery.
For he knows that God is his Saviour.
For there is nothing sweeter than his peace when at rest.

For there is nothing brisker than his life when in motion.

For he is of the Lord's poor, and so indeed is he called by benevolence perpetually—Poor Jeoffry! poor Jeoffry! the rat has bit thy throat.

For I bless the name of the Lord Jesus that Jeoffry is better.

For the divine spirit comes about his body to sustain it in complete cat.

For his tongue is exceeding pure so that it has in purity what it wants in music.

For he is docile and can learn certain things.

For he can sit up with gravity, which is patience upon approbation.

For he can fetch and carry, which is patience in employment.

For he can jump over a stick, which is patience upon proof positive.

For he can spraggle upon waggle at the word of command.

For he can jump from an eminence into his master's bosom.

For he can catch the cork and toss it again.

For he is hated by the hypocrite and miser.

For the former is afraid of detection.

For the latter refuses the charge.

For he camels his back to bear the first notion of business.

For he is good to think on, if a man would express himself neatly.

For he made a great figure in Egypt for his signal services.

For he killed the Icneumon rat, very pernicious by land.

For his ears are so acute that they sting again.

For from this proceeds the passing quickness of his attention.

For by stroking of him I have found out electricity.

For I perceived God's light about him both wax and fire.

For the electrical fire is the spiritual substance which God sends from heaven to sustain the bodies both of man and beast.

For God has blessed him in the variety of his movements.
For, though he cannot fly, he is an excellent clamberer.
For his motions upon the face of the earth are more than
  any other quadruped.
For he can tread to all the measures upon the music.
For he can swim for life.
For he can creep.

GARY SOTO   *(b. 1952)*

At the factory I worked
In the fleck of rubber, under the press
Of an oven yellow with flame,
Until the border patrol opened
Their vans and my boss waved for us to run.
"Over the fence, Soto," he shouted,
And I shouted that I was American.
"No time for lies," he said, and pressed
A dollar in my palm, hurrying me
Through the back door.

Since I was on his time, I ran
And became the wag to a short tail of Mexicans—
Ran past the amazed crowds that lined
The street and blurred like photographs, in rain.
I ran from that industrial road to the soft
Houses where people paled at the turn of an autumn sky.
What could I do but yell *vivas*
To baseball, milkshakes, and those sociologists
Who would clock me
As I jog into the next century
On the power of a great, silly grin.

LEARNING HOW TO LOSE

WILLIAM STAFFORD   *(1914–1993)*

All your years learning how to live to win,
how others judge you, who counts—you know
it's wrong: but those habits cling that brought you
this freedom. You know how to earn it but
you don't know what it is—a friend that you
make is conquered, like an enemy.

Somewhere you'll rest, have faith, even
lose sometimes, accept the way you are, say
easily to the world: "Leave me alone, Hours.
I'm just living here. Let Now win."

ROBERT LOUIS STEVENSON   *(1850–1894)*

Dark brown is the river,
  Golden is the sand.
It flows along for ever,
  With trees on either hand.

Green leaves a-floating,
  Castles of the foam,
Boats of mine a-boating—
  Where will all come home?

On goes the river
  And out past the mill,
Away down the valley,
  Away down the hill.

Away down the river,
  A hundred miles or more,
Other little children
  Shall bring my boats ashore.

GREEN APPLES

RUTH STONE   (b. 1915)

In August we carried the old horsehair mattress
To the back porch
And slept with our children in a row.
The wind came up the mountain into the orchard
Telling me something;
Saying something urgent.
I was happy.
The green apples fell on the sloping roof
And rattled down.
The wind was shaking me all night long;
Shaking me in my sleep
Like a definition of love,
Saying, this is the moment,
Here, now.

RUTH STONE   *(b. 1915)*

Laughter from women gathers like reeds in the river.
A silence of light below their rhythm glazes the water.
They are on a rim of silence looking into the river.
Their laughter traces the water as kingfishers dipping
circles within circles set the reeds clicking;
and an upward rush of herons lifts out of the nests of
    laughter,
their long stick-legs dangling, herons, rising out of the river.

FROM FIREFLIES

RABINDRANATH TAGORE   *(1861–1941)*

The fireflies twinkling among the leaves,
   make the stars wonder.

. . .

Love is an endless mystery,
   for it has nothing else to explain it.

. . .

Let the evening forgive the mistakes of the day
   and thus win peace for herself.

. . .

My last salutations are to them
   who know me imperfect and loved me.

DO NOT GO GENTLE INTO THAT GOOD NIGHT

DYLAN THOMAS   *(1914–1953)*

Do not go gentle into that good night,
Old age should burn and rave at close of day;
Rage, rage against the dying of the light.

Though wise men at their end know dark is right,
Because their words had forked no lightning they
Do not go gentle into that good night.

Good men, the last wave by, crying how bright
Their frail deeds might have danced in a green bay,
Rage, rage against the dying of the light.

Wild men who caught and sang the sun in flight,
And learn, too late, they grieved it on its way,
Do not go gentle into that good night.

Grave men, near death, who see with blinding sight
Blind eyes could blaze like meteors and be gay,
Rage, rage against the dying of the light.

And you, my father, there on the sad height,
Curse, bless, me now with your fierce tears, I pray.
Do not go gentle into that good night.
Rage, rage against the dying of the light.

MARINA TSVETAEVA   (1892–1941)

In my enormous city—night.
From my steep house I go—out,
And people think: wife, daughter—
But I know by heart only one thing: night.

January's wind sweeps clear—the way,
And somewhere from a window a scrap of music—plays.
Ah, the wind today will blow till—dawn
Through the thin chest wall of one to the next.

There's a black poplar tree, and in a window—light,
And the tower chimes, and in my hand—a flower
And this step—goes toward—nobody
And this shadow—though I'm absent.

Lights—like strings of a gold necklace,
My mouth tastes of night's small leaf.
Release me from the bonds of daytime,
Friends, understand; you are dreaming me.

Translated from the Russian by Liz Rosenberg and Nadia Zarembo

MARINA TSVETAEVA   *(1892–1941)*

I like it that you are sick but not with me,
I like it that I am sick, but not with you,
that this heavy ball of earth will never
swim out from under our legs.

I like it that I can be funny—
disheveled—and don't mince words.
And I don't blush in stifling waves
each time you lightly brush my sleeve.

I like it too that when I'm here,
you easily embrace another,
not meaning me to burn
in hellish flames for this.
That my tender name, my tender one, will not
be uttered, day or night—in vain . . .
That never in churchly silence
Will they sing their Hallelujah over us!

Thanks, with heart and hands,
For this: that you—yourself!—don't know
how much you love me, so much: my night's peace
for rare encounters in the sunset hours,
for hours not walking under the moon,
the sun not beating on our heads—
for all of these—that you are sick, alas! and not with me
and I am sick—alas!—not with you!

Translated from the Russian by Liz Rosenberg and Nadia Zarembo

A NOISELESS PATIENT SPIDER

WALT WHITMAN   *(1819–1892)*

A noiseless patient spider,
I mark'd where on a little promontory it stood isolated,
Mark'd how to explore the vacant vast surrounding,
It launch'd forth filament, filament, filament, out of itself,
Ever unreeling them, ever tirelessly speeding them.

And you O my soul where you stand,
Surrounded, detached, in measureless oceans of space,
Ceaselessly musing, venturing, throwing, seeking the spheres
    to connect them,
Till the bridge you will need be form'd, till the ductile
    anchor hold,
    Till the gossamer thread you fling catch somewhere, O
    my soul.

I SAW IN LOUISIANA A LIVE-OAK GROWING

WALT WHITMAN   (1819–1892)

I saw in Louisiana a live-oak growing,
All alone stood it and the moss hung down from the
    branches,
Without any companion it grew there uttering joyous leaves
    of dark green,
And its look, rude, unbending, lusty, made me think of
    myself,
But I wonder'd how it could utter joyous leaves standing
    alone there without its friend near, for I knew I could not,
And I broke off a twig with a certain number of leaves upon
    it, and twined around it a little moss,
And brought it away, and I have placed it in sight in
    my room,
It is not needed to remind me as of my own dear friends,
(For I believe lately I think of little else than of them,)
Yet it remains to me a curious token, it makes me think of
    manly love;
For all that, and though the live-oak glistens there in
    Louisiana solitary in a wide flat space,
Uttering joyous leaves all its life without a friend a
    lover near,
I know very well I could not.

SPARKLES FROM THE WHEEL

WALT WHITMAN   *(1819–1892)*

Where the city's ceaseless crowd moves on the livelong day,
Withdrawn I join a group of children watching—I pause
  aside with them.

By the curb toward the edge of the flagging,
A knife-grinder works at his wheel sharpening a great knife,
Bending over he carefully holds it to the stone—by foot
  and knee,
With measur'd tread he turns rapidly—as he presses with
  light but firm hand,
Forth issue then in copious golden jets,
Sparkles from the wheel.

The scene and all its belongings—how they seize and
  affect me,
The sad sharp-chinn'd old man with worn clothes and broad
  shoulder-band of leather,
Myself effusing and fluid—a phantom curiously floating—
  now here absorb'd and arrested,
The group, (an unminded point set in a vast surrounding,)
The attentive, quiet children—the loud, proud, restive bass
  of the streets,
The low hoarse purr of the whirling stone, the
  light-press'd blade,
Diffusing, dropping, sideways-darting, in tiny showers
  of gold,
Sparkles from the wheel.

I WANDERED LONELY AS A CLOUD

WILLIAM WORDSWORTH   *(1770–1850)*

I wandered lonely as a cloud
That floats on high o'er vales and hills,
When all at once I saw a crowd,
A host, of golden daffodils;
Beside the lake, beneath the trees,
Fluttering and dancing in the breeze.

Continuous as the stars that shine
And twinkle on the milky way,
They stretched in never-ending line
Along the margin of a bay:
Ten thousand saw I at a glance,
Tossing their heads in sprightly dance.

The waves beside them danced; but they
Outdid the sparkling waves in glee;
A poet could not but be gay,
In such a jocund company;
I gazed—and gazed—but little thought
What wealth the show to me had brought:

For oft, when on my couch I lie
In vacant or in pensive mood,
They flash upon that inward eye
Which is the bliss of solitude;
And then my heart with pleasure fills,
And dances with the daffodils.

FROM ODE ON INTIMATIONS OF IMMORTALITY

WILLIAM WORDSWORTH   *(1770–1850)*

Our birth is but a sleep and a forgetting:
The Soul that rises with us, our life's Star,
        Hath had elsewhere its setting,
            And cometh from afar:
        Not in entire forgetfulness,
        And not in utter nakedness,
But trailing clouds of glory do we come
        From God, who is our home:
Heaven lies about us in our infancy!
Shades of the prison-house begin to close
            Upon the growing Boy
                But he
Beholds the light, and whence it flows,
        He sees it in his joy;
The Youth, who daily farther from the east
        Must travel, still is Nature's Priest,
        And by the vision splendid
        Is on his way attended;
At length the Man perceives it die away,
And fade into the light of common day.
· ·
            O joy! that in our embers
            Is something that doth live,
            That nature yet remembers
            What was so fugitive!
The thought of our past years in me doth breed
Perpetual benediction: not indeed
For that which is most worthy to be blest;
Delight and liberty, the simple creed
Of Childhood, whether busy or at rest,

With new-fledged hope still fluttering in his breast—
    Not for these I raise
    The song of thanks and praise;
   But for those obstinate questionings
   Of sense and outward things,
   Fallings from us, vanishings;
   Blank misgivings of a Creature
Moving about in worlds not realized,
High instincts before which our mortal Nature
Did tremble like a guilty Thing surprised;
    But for those first affections,
    Those shadowy recollections,
   Which, be they what they may,
Are yet the fountain light of all our day,
Are yet a master light of all our seeing;
   Uphold us, cherish, and have power to make
Our noisy years seem moments in the being
Of the eternal Silence: truths that wake,
    To perish never;
Which neither listlessness, nor mad endeavor,
    Nor Man nor Boy,
Nor all that is at enmity with joy,
Can utterly abolish or destroy!
    Hence in a season of calm weather
    Though inland far we be,
Our Souls have sight of that immortal sea
    Which brought us hither,
    Can in a moment travel thither,
And see the Children sport upon the shore,
And hear the mighty waters rolling evermore.
Then sing, ye Birds, sing, sing a joyous song!
    And let the young Lambs bound
    As to the tabor's sound!
We in thought will join your throng,
    Ye that pipe and ye that play,

Ye that through your hearts today
Feel the gladness of the May!
What though the radiance which was once so bright
Be now forever taken from my sight,
Though nothing can bring back the hour
Of splendor in the grass, of glory in the flower;
We will grieve not, rather find
Strength in what remains behind;
In the primal sympathy
Which having been must ever be;
In the soothing thoughts that spring
Out of human suffering;
In the faith that looks through death,
In years that bring the philosophic mind.

And O, ye Fountains, Meadows, Hills, and Groves,
Forebode not any severing of our loves!
Yet in my heart of hearts I feel your might;
I only have relinquished one delight
To live beneath your more habitual sway.
I love the Brooks which down their channels fret,
Even more than when I tripped lightly as they;
The innocent brightness of a newborn Day
Is lovely yet;
The clouds that gather round the setting sun
Do take a sober coloring from an eye
That hath kept watch o'er man's mortality;
Another race hath been, and other palms are won.
Thanks to the human heart by which we live,
Thanks to its tenderness, its joys, and fears,
To me the meanest* flower that blows† can give
Thoughts that do often lie too deep for tears.

*plainest
†blooms

THE LAKE ISLE OF INNISFREE

WILLIAM BUTLER YEATS   *(1865 — 1939)*

I will arise and go now, and go to Innisfree,
And a small cabin build there, of clay and wattles made:
Nine bean rows will I have there, a hive for the honey bee,
And live alone in the bee-loud glade.

And I shall have some peace there, for peace comes
      dropping slow,
Dropping from the veils of the morning to where the
      cricket sings;
There midnight's all a glimmer, and noon a purple glow,
And evening full of the linnet's wings.

I will arise and go now, for always night and day
I hear lake water lapping with low sounds by the shore;
While I stand on the roadway, or on the pavements gray,
I hear it in the deep heart's core.

THE FIDDLER OF DOONEY

WILLIAM BUTLER YEATS   *(1865–1939)*

When I play on my fiddle in Dooney,
Folk dance like a wave of the sea;
My cousin is priest in Kilvarnet,
My brother in Moharabuiee.

I passed my brother and cousin:
They read in their books of prayer;
I read in my book of songs
I bought at the Sligo fair.

When we come at the end of time
To Peter sitting in state,
He will smile on the three old spirits,
But call me first through the gate;

For the good are always the merry,
Save by an evil chance,
And the merry love the fiddle
And the merry love to dance:

And when the folk there spy me,
They will all come up to me,
With 'Here is the fiddler of Dooney!'
And dance like a wave of the sea.

AFRICAN-AMERICAN ANONYMOUS POET (1800s): The author of "Follow the Drinking Gourd" is unknown, but we can guess that this African-American spiritual, about escape to freedom, was sung during the time of slavery down South, probably the early to middle 1800s.

We know, too, that Peg Leg Joe was a real person, an elderly man who worked as an itinerant carpenter, spending his winters moving from plantation to plantation, teaching slaves in Alabama and Mississippi how to escape north by means of this coded song.

"The drinking gourd" is another name for the Big Dipper, that starry constellation whose handle points due north, toward the North Star. "Follow the Drinking Gourd" gives specific geographical clues on the route north (hills, rivers). Of all the escape routes out of the Deep South, this is one of a very few for which the details survive.

SUGGESTED READING: *All Night, All Day: A Children's First Book of African-American Spirituals* (edited by Ashley Bryan, photographs by David Manning Thomas; Atheneum).

Go Down, Moses: A Celebration of African-American Spirituals (edited by Richard Newman, et al.; Clarkson Potter).

CHARLES BAUDELAIRE (1821–1867) was born in Paris to a well-to-do and respected family. Almost from the start, Baudelaire was a "problem child." Early on, he was expelled from school. He wanted to live by his writing, but under pressure became a law student. He spent much of this time in dissipation, and ran into debt and trouble with alcohol, opium, and women. He became involved in radical French politics, but grew more and more conservative over time. He published poems, novels, and essays on art, and translated and introduced to Europe the works of Edgar Allen Poe. Some of his poems are written in classic, rhyming forms; others (like "The Bad Glazier") are prose poems. He is considered the founder of the French Symbolist movement, whose followers, such as Verlaine and Rimbaud, sought to "derange" meaning, and wrote about gritty, urban, decadent life, and the life of dreams. "Genius," he once wrote, "is childhood recaptured."

SUGGESTED READING: *Baudelaire: Poems* (Everyman's Pocket Edition, Knopf).

Baudelaire, Rimbaud and Verlaine: Selected Poems and Prose Poems (edited by Joseph M. Bernstein; Citadel Press).

Paris Spleen (prose poems translated by Louise Varèse; New Directions).

STEVEN BAUER (b. 1948) was born in Newark, New Jersey, on September 10. He grew up in northern New Jersey, went to school in Connecticut, and has worked in a health food store, a grocery, and a country club, as well as teaching in numerous colleges in New England and elsewhere. He now directs the Creative Writing Program at Miami University in Oxford, Ohio, where he lives with his wife, the writer Liz Arthur, and their two dogs. Bauer recently published his first picture book, and his new middle-grade novel will be coming out this fall. He loves to cook and to garden, and he loves animals.

SUGGESTED READING: *Daylight Savings* (Peregrine Smith Books).

The Strange and Wonderful Tale of Robert McDoodle (The Boy Who Wanted to Be a Dog) (illustrations by Brad Sneed; Simon & Schuster).

A Cat of a Different Color (Random House).

GWENDOLYN B. BENNETT (1902–1981) grew up on an Indian reservation in Nevada. Her parents divorced when she was eight, and though her mother won custody her father kidnapped her, moving her from place to place till Bennett was a teenager. She attended Columbia University and then taught art at Howard University. She was involved in the Harlem Renaissance as poet, dancer, artist, and for a brief time as columnist for the black magazine *Opportunity*, before she and her husband, Dr. Alfred Jackson, moved to Florida in 1928. She died in obscurity, though she had been a vibrant part of the Harlem Renaissance fifty years earlier. Catherine Clinton writes, "Bennett did not produce a large body of work, but with other younger artists of the Renaissance, she had a meteoric impact that helped change attitudes toward African Americans."

SUGGESTED READING: *The Harlem Renaissance and Beyond: Literary Biographies of 100 Black Women Writers, 1900–1945* (edited by Lorraine Elena Roses and Ruth Elizabeth Randolph; Harvard University Press).

I, Too, Sing America: Three Centuries of African-American Poetry (edited by Catherine Clinton, illustrated by Stephen Alcorn; Houghton Mifflin).

The Sleeper Awakes: Harlem Renaissance Stories by Women (Rutgers University Press).

See also a Web site called *Poetry and Prose of the Harlem Renaissance*.

WILLIAM BLAKE (1757–1827), born on November 28, was a visionary even as a child—he saw angels in the tree by his house—and, at least according to his wife, Katherine, continued to speak with her in their garden after his death. As a child, Blake was sent to drawing school, began writing poetry at age twelve, and at fourteen became apprenticed to an engraver. He studied briefly at the British Royal Academy, but rebelled against the academic doctrines—especially those of its president, the painter Sir Joshua Reynolds. Blake eked out a living (sometimes barely) as an engraver and illustrator.

Ignored, even ridiculed most of his life, he nonetheless worked on both his poetry and his art—with poems and illustrations often engraved together on copper plates, by a process Blake claimed had been dictated to him by angels. He sometimes suffered a "Deep pit of Melancholy," but would sign his letters "Enthusiastic, hope-fostered visionary." His poetry, satires, annotations on the works of others, letters, fragments, and sayings from *The Marriage of Heaven and Hell* still have fresh power to startle or delight us: "Always be ready to speak your mind, and a base man will avoid you"; "Exuberance is beauty"; "What is now proved was once only imagin'd."

SUGGESTED READING: *Blake: Complete Writings* (edited by Geoffrey Keynes, this book includes all the poems, letters, annotations, notes, and is indispensable for any true lover of Blake; Oxford University Press).

Songs of Innocence and of Experience (presents a perfect example of Blake's illuminated art; Oxford University Press).

ELIZABETH BARRETT BROWNING (1806–1861) was born in Durham, England, where she and her siblings led a well-to-do but much sequestered life. Elizabeth was considered an invalid, too weak to go out into the world, and certainly, her father felt, far too delicate for romance or marriage. Nonetheless the younger poet Robert Browning began writing admiring letters to Elizabeth about her poetry. This correspondence turned at length into a serious romance—which was bitterly opposed by her father. In 1846 Elizabeth and Robert eloped and settled in Florence, Italy. Though best known for her love poems—particularly the *Sonnets from the Portuguese*, written for Robert during their long courtship (carried on mostly by letter and rare, secret meetings)—she also wrote the long poem, *Aurora Leigh,* which defends a woman's right to intellectual freedom and to the free exercise of her own art.

SUGGESTED: *Aurora Leigh and Other Poems* (edited by John Robert G. Bolton; Penguin Classics, Penguin Books).

Sonnets from the Portuguese and Other Love Poems (revised edition, Doubleday; contains the forty-four interlocking sonnets written for Robert, plus twenty-two more; also available on audiocassette from Spoken Arts).

GEORGE GORDON, LORD BYRON (1788–1823) acquired the title of baron quite unexpectedly at the age of ten, when his great-uncle died and left him a title and a castle given to the Byrons by Henry VIII. Lord Byron lived a dramatic, often scandalous life, and despite the club foot he was born with—and about which he was extremely sensitive—he was renowned as a dashing and romantic figure. When his first book of poems, *Hours of Idleness,* was published in 1807, it was savaged by *The Edinburgh Review* (see John Keats). He responded with satiric couplets titled *English Bards and Scotch Reviewers*, which earned him his first literary recognition. The first two cantos of his poem *Childe Harold* sold out within a few days. ("I awoke one morning and found myself famous," Byron remarked.) He spoke twice in the House of Lords; swam a mile in the dangerous waters between Europe and eastern Turkey; was expelled from Ravenna, Italy, for taking part in a failed revolutionary uprising; and traveled through Portugal, Spain, Turkey, and Greece, where he sailed in 1823 to help fight for that country's independence. Before he ever entered into battle, however, he was struck by a fever, and died at age thirty-five. He immediately became a Greek national hero, but his body was refused burial in Westminster Abbey until nearly one hundred fifty years after his death. He wrote in a letter to John Murray, "I am like the tyger (in poesy), if I miss my first Spring, I go growling back to my Jungle. There is no second. I can't correct; I can't, and I won't."

SUGGESTED READING: *Selected Poems* (Dover Thrift Editions).

Selected Poetry of George Gordon Byron (edited by Jerome J. McGann; Oxford World's Classics, Oxford University Press).

CHOSU is a Japanese poet about whom no information was readily available. His translator, **Harry Behn** (1898–1973), wrote poems and stories for both children and adults, and his poetry is widely anthologized.

SUGGESTED READING: *Cricket Songs* (Japanese haiku compiled by Harry Behn; Harcourt, Brace and World).

More Cricket Songs (Japanese haiku translated by Harry Behn; Harcourt, Brace, Jovanovich).

SAMUEL TAYLOR COLERIDGE (1772–1834): Born the son of a poor clergyman, Coleridge was sent at the age of ten from his rural home in Devonshire to a boy's harsh charity school in London, where his only friend was his classmate, the poet and storyteller Charles Lamb. He entered Jesus College, Cambridge, in 1791, but left to enlist as a dragoon under the unlikely pseudonym Silas Tomkyn Cumberback. (Luckily, his family found him out at the last minute.) He and the poet Robert Southey tried to found a utopian "Pantisocracy" on the banks of the Susquehanna River in Pennsylvania, but when those plans fell through, he remained engaged to Southey's sister Sara, whom he married, without much joy on either side. His greatest happiness may well have come from his long, close friendship with the poet William Wordsworth and Wordsworth's sister, Dorothy. Together he and Wordsworth published the *Lyrical Ballads of 1798*, which revolutionized poetry at the time, and set forth some of the main principles of Romantic poetry. Coleridge's health was never good, and he suffered all his life from stomach pains, which were treated early on with opiates, to which he eventually became addicted. Yet while he worked, lectured, and wrote, he was known as one of the greatest minds and most brilliant speakers of his time. The writer William Hazlitt recalled that "His voice rolled on the ear like the pealing organ, and its sound alone was the music of thought. His mind was clothed with wings; and raised on them, he lifted philosophy to heaven." When his childhood friend Charles Lamb heard of Coleridge's death he wrote, "His great and dear spirit haunts me. . . . He was the proof and touchstone of all my cogitations."

SUGGESTED READING: *The Portable Coleridge* (edited and with an introduction by I. A. Richards; Viking Press).

BILLY COLLINS (b. 1952) lives in Somers, New York, and is the author of six books of poetry. His work has been featured on *The Prairie Home Companion* and on a CD/cassette of his poems, *The Best Cigarette*. Collins is sometimes known for the wit and humor of his poetry, but his work has more facets than that; among other interests revealed in his poetry are those in zen, art, history, jazz, and blues. A professor of English at Lehman College in the City University of New York, he has for years conducted summer writing workshops in Ireland at the University College, Galway, and was poet-in-residence at Burren College of Art in Ireland.

SUGGESTED: *The Best Cigarette* (award-winning CD/cassette featuring Collins reading more than thirty of his poems; Cielo Vivo Press).

Picnic, Lightning (Pitt Poetry Series, Pittsburgh).

Questions About Angels (selected by Edward Hirsch as a winner of the National Poetry Series; Pitt Poetry Series, Pittsburgh).

JAMES DICKEY (1923–1997) was born in Atlanta, Georgia, the youngest of three children and only surviving son. He attended Vanderbilt University between two military stints as a night flier in the U.S. Air Force, and worked for a time as a successful advertising executive—"selling his soul to the devil in the daytime and buying it back at night," he said. He read one of his poems at President Jimmy Carter's inauguration, won a National Book Award for his book of poems, *Buck-dancer's Choice,* and the French Prix Médicis for his novel *Deliverance*, which was adapted into a movie in which he made a cameo appearance.

Hesitant and shy at first at his poetry readings, he began carrying around a guitar "to make myself seem more interesting," and eventually became one of the most charismatic and provocative literary figures of his time. He was a poet, novelist, essayist, reviewer, writer of children's books, musician, hunter, and for many years a professor and poet-in-residence at the University of South Carolina in Columbia. Though he could be rough and bearlike, he was also known for his generosity to students and countless young writers. In one of his poems he prays for "a little more kindness, Lord."

SUGGESTED READING: *Poems 1957–1967* (Wesleyan University Press).

Self-Interviews (Doubleday).

EMILY DICKINSON (1830–1886) was born on December 10, in Amherst, Massachusetts, where she spent almost every day of her life. Toward the end of her life she spent her time in the seclusion of her house, often locked in her room. "One turn of the key," she once confided to a close friend, "and—freedom, Maddie!" She attended the Amherst Academy and, briefly, the Mount Holyoke Female Seminary in South Hadley, Massachusetts. Nonetheless, she carried on lively and literary correspondence, first with the well-known Boston editor Thomas Higginson to whom she wrote in 1862, asking, "Are you too deeply occupied to say if my verse is alive?" Later she kept a constant exchange of poems and letters with her beloved sister-in-law Sue. Though she is sometimes seen as a grim or pristine spinster, she told Higginson her companions were "Hills, sir, and the sundown, and a dog large as myself, that my father bought me," and that "the mere sense of living is joy enough." She published less than a handful of poems in her lifetime—chiefly in the local newspaper—and declined an invitation to publish a volume of her verse. Poet Adrienne Rich has written of Dickinson "that genius knows itself; that Dickinson chose her seclusion, knowing she was exceptional and knowing what was needed."

Though her work was published posthumously—she had written some two thousand poems, on small pieces of paper, some of them carefully bound and sewn—the work was "fixed" by Higginson and her brother's lover, Mabel Loomis Todd, a literary woman who had only glimpsed Dickinson once, through a doorway. They changed her punctuation, spelling, sometimes adjusted words and rhymes. Her work, as written, was not published till Thomas H. Johnson's definitive edition in 1955, nearly seventy years after her death.

SUGGESTED READING: *The Complete Poems of Emily Dickinson* (edited by Thomas H. Johnson; Little, Brown).

On Lies, Secrets, and Silence: Selected Prose 1966–1978 (by Adrienne Rich; includes the fine essay, "Vesuvius at Home: The Power of Emily Dickinson"; Norton).

NOTE: The answer to the riddle poem is a hummingbird.

H.D. (HILDA DOOLITTLE) (1884–1961) was born to a wealthy family in Pennsylvania, not far from the poet Ezra Pound, who became her first love, editor, secret fiancé, and, after the collapse of the romance, lifelong friend: a complex love story heartrendingly told by H.D. in her memoir, *End to Torment*. For too long H.D. has been known merely as an appendage to Pound, one of his group of so-called "Imagists." While it is true that some of her poems fit many of the Imagist rules (the presentation of "the thing in itself," little embellishment, intense imagery), she also wrote translations from the ancient Greek, long, philosophical and experimental poems, like *Helen in Egypt*, the memoir on Pound, and a memoir on Sigmund Freud. She is also considered one of the century's most important feminist poets.

SUGGESTED READING: *End to Torment: A Memoir of Ezra Pound* (New Directions).

H.D. Selected Poems (edited by Louis L. Martz; New Directions).

Collected Poems: 1912–1944 (edited by Louis L. Martz; New Directions).

ROBERT FROST (1874–1963) was born in San Francisco, and lived there until he was eleven, though he is best known as the ultimate American poet of New England rural life. He moved to New England after his father's death, and lived with his mother and grandparents. He studied classics in high school, entered and dropped out of both Harvard and Dartmouth, and worked at various times as a schoolteacher, a farmer, and one of America's most beloved poets. He was the first poet of the twentieth century to read a poem at a presidential inauguration (John F. Kennedy's), which he did when he was well into his eighties. It is said that it was while he was laboring without success on that poem ("The Gift Outright") the poem "Stopping by Woods on a Snowy Evening" suddenly came to him. His grave is in Old Bennington, Vermont, in a churchyard. The gravestone reads, "I had a lover's quarrel with the world."

SUGGESTED READING: *The Poetry of Robert Frost* (Henry Holt).

You Come, Too: Favorite Poems for Young Readers by Robert Frost (wood engravings by Thomas W. Nason; Henry Holt).

A Restless Spirit: A Biography of Robert Frost (by Natalie S. Bober; Henry Holt).

Selected Prose of Robert Frost (edited by Hyde Cox and Edward Connery Lathem; Henry Holt).

MARIA MAZZIOTTI GILLAN (b. 1943) was born to parents who immigrated to the United States from southern Italy. She founded and directs the Poetry Center at Passaic Community College, which sponsors poetry readings, prizes, conferences, and poetry in the public schools of New Jersey. She has published seven books of poems, and together with her daughter, Jennifer Gillan, has coedited two anthologies, *Unsettling America* and *Identity Lessons*. She has appeared on National Public Radio's *All Things Considered*, and Garrison Keillor's *Writer's Almanac*. She is at work on a memoir called *My Mother's Stoop*.

SUGGESTED READING: *Identity Lessons: Contemporary Writing About Learning to Be American* (coedited by Jennifer Gillan and Maria Mazziotti Gillan; Penguin Books).

Things My Mother Told Me (Guernica Editions).

Unsettling America: An Anthology of Contemporary Multicultural Poetry (coedited by Jennifer Gillan and Maria Mazziotti Gillan; Penguin Books).

Where I Come From: Selected and New Poems (Guernica Editions).

ALLEN GINSBERG (1926–1997) was born and raised in Paterson, New Jersey, son of the poet Louis Ginsberg and Naomi Ginsberg, who had a breakdown when Allen was a young teenager; he was the one who took her by bus to an asylum. This harrowing story of love and sorrow is told in his long, powerful poem *Kaddish*, which he wrote in thirty-six hours. Ginsberg and other writers of the so-called Beat Generation gathered around Columbia University in the mid-1940s. They were known for their raw honesty, experimentation in life as well as art, and rejection of middle-class standards and values. Ginsberg, who lived an openly gay life, broke any number of taboos in the forties, fifties, sixties—indeed right until his death. He was an outspoken political activist; a practicing Buddhist (and Jew); a teacher and photographer, as well as a lyricist and musician who performed with Bob Dylan and others. His goal, he once told an interviewer, was to be "a self-possessed Master of the Universe." Once, in his early twenties, he heard the voice of the visionary poet William Blake reciting Blake's poem "Ah, Sunflower" to him—an experience he vowed never to refute, forget, or deny—and never did.

His poems range from the book-length, breakthrough poems like *Kaddish* and *Howl* to tiny dated notations and one-line haiku. When asked by someone what he believed future generations would think of him, he answered, "That's none of my business."

SUGGESTED READING: *Collected Poems 1947–1980* (Harper and Row).

Kaddish and Other Poems (City Lights Books).

MICHAEL S. GLASER (b. 1943) works with many young readers and writers of poetry through the Maryland State Arts Council's Poet-in-the-Schools program, as well as through teaching summer youth courses at St. Mary's College of Maryland, where he is the chair of the English Department. His poems have appeared in many literary and scholarly journals, anthologies, and newspapers, including a chapbook, *In the Men's Room and Other Poems,* and his collection, *A Lover's Eye.* Michael lives in St. Mary's City with his wife, Kathleen, and is the proud father of five children.

SUGGESTED READING: *Lover's Eye* (Poe-General Publishers).

ANGELINA WELD GRIMKÉ (1880–1958) was the daughter of a prominent black clergyman in Boston and a white mother who abandoned her when she was still a child. She was named after her father's famous aunt, Angelina Grimké Weld, who, with her sister Susan, worked as a pioneer first for abolition and then for women's suffrage. Angelina Grimké, the poet, became an English teacher in Washington, D.C., and wrote poems and plays. Though well-known in her time, she died in relative obscurity in 1958, and is only now beginning to regain the reputation she deserves as a poet and female artist in the Harlem Renaissance.

SUGGESTED READING: *The Harlem Renaissance and Beyond: Literary Biographies of 100 Black Women Writers, 1900–1945* (edited by Lorraine Elena Roses and Ruth Elizabeth Randolph; Harvard University Press).

I, Too, Sing America: Three Centuries of African-American Poetry (edited by Catherine Clinton, illustrated by Stephen Alcorn; Houghton Mifflin).

The Sleeper Awakes: Harlem Renaissance Stories by Women (Rutgers University Press).

Voices from the Harlem Renaissance (edited by Nathan Irwin Huggins; Oxford University Press).

See also a Web site called *Poetry and Prose of the Harlem Renaissance.*

ROBERT HAYDEN (1913–1980) grew up in the Detroit slums, an experience often reflected in his poetry, along with poems about African-American history and African-American figures such as Nat Turner and Frederick Douglass, as well as elegies for Robert Kennedy and Martin Luther King. Hayden was a fellow of the American Academy of Poets, served as poetry consultant to the Library of Congress, and stayed steadfastly independent of all poetic schools and movements.

SUGGESTED READING: *Collected Poems of Robert Hayden* (Liveright Publishers).

Angle of Ascent (Liveright Publishers).

Collected Prose (University of Michigan Press).

WILLIAM ERNEST HENLEY (1849–1903) was born in Gloucester, England, first of six children born to a struggling bookseller and his wife. He left grammar school early because of his family's poverty and his own ill health. In childhood he had a disease that resulted in the partial amputation of one leg when he was a teenager. He became a poet, essayist, and editor, and also collaborated with his best friend, Robert Louis Stevenson, on four plays. It is thought that the character Long John Silver in *Treasure Island* is based on Henley. Stevenson said Henley's "presence could be felt in a room if you entered it blindfolded."

SUGGESTED READING: *Lyra Heroica* (Ayer Co.).
The Works of William Ernest Henley (out of print).

GEORGE HERBERT (1593–1633) was born to Richard Herbert of Montgomery Castle, England. His father died when George was four, and his mother moved the family to Oxford, where the poet was educated at home until he was twenty-two years old. He then attended Westminster School and Trinity College, Cambridge, and became a well-known public orator there, a popular and elegant courtier. He hoped for a political career, but his mother and her good friend—the poet John Donne—urged him to take religious orders. Herbert felt he had little calling for a holy life, but nonetheless withdrew from Cambridge and lived quietly in Kent, trying to decide his future. In this environment he fell ill and was in danger of tuberculosis (called consumption at the time; see John Keats, below), but during this time he met and married his cousin, Jane Danvers. Sometime before their wedding Herbert had become an Anglican priest and began to write the sacred poems for which he is known. (He destroyed the manuscript of all his secular poems when he became a priest.) He was known to his contemporaries as "a saint, unspotted of the world, full of alms-deeds," and his last act before his death was to play and sing one of his poems, "The Sundays of Man's Life."

SUGGESTED READING: *The Complete English Poems of George Herbert* (edited by John Tobin; Penguin Books).

MARIE HOWE (b. 1950) was for a number of years a public high school teacher before earning her M.F.A. in Creative Writing from Columbia University in 1983. She has taught at Tufts University, Dartmouth College, New York University, Sarah Lawrence College, and Columbia University, and lives part of the year in Provincetown, Massachusetts, and part of the year in New York City. In addition to her two books of poems, she also edited, with Michael Klein, an anthology called *In the Company of My Solitude: American Writing from the AIDS Pandemic.*

SUGGESTED READING: *The Good Thief* (selected for the National Poetry Series by Margaret Atwood; Persea Books).

What the Living Do (W.W. Norton).

LANGSTON HUGHES (1902–1967) was born on February 1, in Joplin, Missouri, son of a lawyer (his father) and a teacher (his mother). His father left the family before Langston was two, and before the boy was twelve years old he had lived in seven different cities in the United States. After high school, he spent a year in Mexico with his father, then a year at Columbia University, and finished his B.A. at Lincoln University, Pennsylvania. He traveled all over the world, and worked at everything from waiter to truck driver to ship's mess boy to journalist. He wrote short stories, blues lyrics, humor, children's books, plays, essays, autobiography, as well as poems in rhyme or blues rhythms or spoken aloud to jazz, and lectured widely, on his life, his work, and his desire for social justice. He was a dynamic figure in the Harlem Renaissance movement, a spokesman for civil rights, and an indefatigable optimist. His poetry tells us, "Hold fast to dreams."

SUGGESTED READING: *Shimmy Shimmy Shimmy Like My Sister Kate: Looking at the Harlem Renaissance Through Poems* (by Nikki Giovanni; Henry Holt).

The Dream Keeper and Other Poems (illustrated by Brian Pinkney, with an introduction by Lee Bennett Hopkins; Knopf).

LEIGH HUNT (1784–1859) born at Southgate, England, was the son of a Barbados clergyman and an American mother. His health as a child was very poor, but at seven he was sent to Christ Church School, where he began to write poetry. He published a volume called *Juvenalia* while he was still a teenager. He worked as a drama critic, a clerk in the War Office, and editor of a British newspaper. For rudeness to the Prince Regent, Hunt was jailed for two years, and it was during this time he began to write in earnest, and became friends with fellow poets Keats, Shelley, and Byron, especially after he had settled at Hampstead, near Keats. He edited one newspaper after another—all of them failures, and most written entirely by Hunt himself. He also published a novel, poems, and in 1840 finally had a real success with his play, *A Legend of Florence*. In 1847 he received a royal pension, which kept him free of money worries for the rest of his life. He said that he spent his later years "reading or writing, ailing, jesting, reflecting, rarely stirring from home but to walk, interested in public events, in the progress of society, in things great or small, in the flower on my table, in the fly on my paper as I write."

SUGGESTED READING: *Selected Writings by Leigh Hunt* (Scholarly Book Services).

DAVID IGNATOW (1914–1997) was born in Brooklyn, and spent most of his life in and around the New York metropolis, working both as poet and as editor of *The American Poetry Review*, the *Beloit Poetry Journal*, as poetry editor at *The Nation*, and as coeditor of *Chelsea*. He taught at a number of universities, served as president of the Poetry Society of America, and, in one of his poems, urged us all to reach out and "rescue the dead." He published seventeen books of poetry, including the posthumous *At My Ease: Uncollected Poems of the Fifties and Sixties*.

SUGGESTED READING: *Against the Evidence: Selected Poems 1934–1994* (Wesleyan University Press).

Letters 1946–1990 (Wesleyan University Press).

ISSA (or ISSA KOBAYASHI) (1763–1827) experienced many tragedies in his life, yet he remains one of the most compassionate and hopeful of all Japanese poets. His mother died when he was two, and he was sent out on an apprenticeship to Tokyo (then known as Edo) when he was only fourteen. He spent much of his life wandering around the country, writing haiku (short three-line poems) and haibun (travel notebooks that contain poems at key moments). When he was nearly middle aged his dying father begged him to marry and settle down in his old village. True to his word, Issa did just that, living in one half of his father's house (his widowed stepmother and stepbrother kept the other) and marrying a local girl. Their first four children all died young, but a fifth daughter outlived him. An aspiring Buddhist, Issa regarded all living things with tenderness and gentle humor, addressing a spider in his house, for instance, telling it not to worry, "I keep house / casually."

SUGGESTED READING: *The Essential Haiku: Versions of Bashō, Buson, and Issa* (edited by Robert Hass; Ecco Press).

The Spring of My Life and Selected Poems by Issa Kobayashi (this is the diary of a year in which one of Issa's young daughters died, plus a selection of his poems; translated by Sam Hamill, illustrated by Kaji Asso; Shambhala Press).

ROLF JACOBSEN (1907–1994) was born in Oslo, Norway. At the age of six he moved to the countryside where, he later wrote, "I went through a second birth." He worked for many years as a local journalist in Hamar, northeast of Oslo. After his first two books of poems were published, he waited nearly fifteen years to publish the third—which was followed by succeeding books every three or four years thereafter. In 1985 *Night Open* (which contains the poem "Look") was a bestseller in Norway.
SUGGESTED READING: *Night Open: Selected Poems of Rolf Jacobsen* (translated by Olav Grinde; White Pine Press).

VICKIE KARP (b. 1953) was born in New York City, and educated at Queens College of the City University of New York. She has worked as a teacher, an editor at *The New Yorker*, and is currently a senior writer for public television. In addition to her book of poems, *A Taxi to the Flame*, Ms. Karp has written documentaries about Marianne Moore, Dorothy Parker, and Ernest Hemingway, and a play based on the writings of the poet Elizabeth Bishop.
SUGGESTED READING: *A Taxi to the Flame: Poems by Vickie Karp* (University of South Carolina Press).

JOHN KEATS (1795–1821) was born in late October, in the stable of the Swan and Hoop Inn in England. He was a brave and fiery-tempered child, known "as a pet prize-fighter, for his terrier courage." His father died when he was nine; his mother, when he was fifteen. His guardian removed him from school at this point, and sent him to work as an apprentice surgeon for five years. He never liked medicine, however, and at the age of seventeen began to write poems. In March 1817 he published his first book, *Poems,* a total failure. He began working on his long poem, "Endymion," and moved to Hampstead with his brothers. It was in Hampstead that he fell in love with and became secretly engaged to Fanny Brawne, the daughter of his landlady. Always delicate in health, Keats became so ill climbing a mountain on a walking tour of the Lake Country and Scotland that his doctor forbade him ever to travel again; at this time not only was his poem "Endymion" brutally reviewed in the influential literary magazines the *Quarterly Review* and *Blackwood's*, but his beloved younger brother Tom was dying of tuberculosis (known then as "consumption"). Keats himself moved to London, looking for work, then moved back to Hampstead to be near Fanny Brawne. During the winter of 1820 he took a long, bitterly cold ride on the top of a coach because he could not afford a seat inside, and soon after found blood on his pillow, recognizing at once that he too was dying of consumption. The poet Shelley, hearing of his distress, invited Keats to spend the winter in Italy, but Keats declined the invitation, later traveling with his friend the painter Joseph Severn, first to Naples, then to Rome, where he died in February 1821 at the age of twenty-five. He left behind an amazing body of work: letters, long poems, sonnets, and his beautiful odes. In a letter to his friend Benjamin Bailey, he wrote, "I am certain of nothing but of the holiness of the Heart's affections and the truth of Imagination—."

SUGGESTED READING: *The Essential Keats* (selected by Philip Levine; Ecco Press).

JANE KENYON (1947–1995) was born in Ann Arbor, Michigan, where she lived on the outskirts of town, and attended a one-room school through the fourth grade. She began writing poems during junior high school and was still working on her poetry one month before she died. During her lifetime she published four collections of poetry, taught, and translated the poetry of the great Russian poet Anna Akhmatova. She and her husband, the poet Donald Hall, moved to his family's old farmstead, Eagle Pond Farm, in New Hampshire, where she lived a full and busy life, gardened, and wrote. She suffered much of her life from bouts of depression, an experience she records in some of her most powerful poems. Her husband has written, "Her readers are aware of Jane's struggles with depression—and also of her joy in the body and creation, in flowers, music, and paintings, in hayfields and a dog."

SUGGESTED: *Otherwise: New and Selected Poems* (Graywolf Press).

Twenty Poems of Anna Akhmatova (translated by Jane Kenyon; Eighties Press).

A Hundred White Daffodils (translations, interviews, and prose; Graywolf Press).

"A Life Together," which aired on PBS as part of *Bill Moyers' Journal*, won an Emmy in 1994 and is available on video from *Films for the Humanities and Sciences* (800-257-5126).

OMAR KHAYYÁM and his translator, **EDWARD FITZGERALD:** Omar Khayyám, whose name means "Omar the Tentmaker" (probably his father's profession), lived from the mid-eleventh century to 1123. He was well-known as a Persian poet, scientist, astronomer, and author of an algebra that was still being translated into English in the mid-nineteenth century. Considered the leading mathematician of his time, he authored many scholarly works and was appointed to a commission that reformed the Persian calendar. Edward Fitz-Gerald drew heightened attention to *The Rubáiyát* with his interpretation of the poems, published in 1859, and enthusiastically praised by the poet Dante Gabriel Rossetti (Christina's brother). FitzGerald played fast and loose with the Persian original, giving it a distinctly nineteenth-century British tone while creating a seemingly whole poem out of separate, epigrammatic quatrains. What we really have, then, is a beautiful collaboration of two poets working together across seven centuries, two languages, and three continents.

SUGGESTED READING: There are many editions of *The Rubáiyát* currently available, several of them beautifully illustrated. My personal favorite is the Peter Pauper Edition, a small, inexpensive edition with illustrations by Paul McPharlin.

Dover Thrift Editions, a wonderful series of public domain titles (books gone out of copyright), offers an even cheaper paperback edition for only one dollar.

DAS LANZILLOTTI (b. 1950) was born of immigrant parents (an Italian mother and Argentine father). He grew up in rural New Jersey, surrounded by dairy cattle, and he has written that before he began school "my only friends were cows and their calves." He attended Cooper Union, completed several apprenticeships in sculpture, married young, and has two children. He has lived in South America, Mexico, and in many deserts, and now divides his time between New Mexico and Florida. He writes, "My poetry has always been simple and almost always 'peasantlike.'" In addition to poetry, painting, and sculpture, he makes handcrafted jewelry, which has been displayed all over the United States and has won numerous prizes.

DAVID HERBERT (D. H.) LAWRENCE (1885–1930) was born and raised in Nottinghamshire, England, the fourth of five children of a hardworking miner and his wife. During his adult life Lawrence moved all over Europe, to Ceylon, Australia, and, at the end of his life, New Mexico. Well-known as the author of controversial novels such as *Sons and Lovers* and *Women in Love*, he also wrote poems, plays, essays, translations, and stories. His last novel, *Lady Chatterley's Lover,* was banned in England in 1928; the next year his paintings were confiscated. Lawrence was diagnosed with tuberculosis at twenty-six, but he managed to live a full, if abbreviated, life; he died in 1930, in Venice, at age forty-four. His wife, Frieda, wrote of him, "What he had seen and felt and known he gave in his writing to his fellow men, the splendor of living, the hope of more and more life. . . ."

SUGGESTED READING: *The Complete Poems of D. H. Lawrence* (collected and edited with an introduction and notes by Vivian de Sola Pinto and Warren Roberts; Penguin Books).

D. H. Lawrence: Selected Poetry (selected and introduced by Keith Sagar; Penguin Books).

EDNA ST. VINCENT MILLAY (1892–1950)—nicknamed Vincent or Vince—was born in Maine, one of three sisters. When she was seven, her parents separated, and Edna, her sisters, and mother lived together in a tight-knit family circle, where Millay's mother encouraged them all in music, literature, theatricals, and dance. Millay later wrote to her mother, "I can not remember once in my life when you were not interested in what I was working on, or even suggested I should put it aside for something else." Millay became the first woman to win the Pulitzer Prize in Poetry, for *The Harp-Weaver and Other Poems*, published while she was still at Vassar College on scholarship. After graduating, she spent time in Provincetown, writing and acting for the famous Provincetown Players, and later living a "bohemian" life in Greenwich Village. Complex, intense, relentlessly inventive in both her work and life, she has too long been branded either a glamorous playgirl or an old-fashioned lady who wrote quaint, rhymed verse. In 1923 she married Eugen Boissevain. Together they moved to a farm, Steepletop, in Austerlitz, New York. In 1975 her sister Norma established the Millay Colony for the Arts, still in existence. Millay's sonnets are among the best examples of the form in the twentieth century, and her political activism and social conscience are demonstrated in many of her poems, plays, and satirical sketches. She may have "burned her candle at both ends" too brilliantly, for she died at age fifty-six, one year after the death of her husband.

SUGGESTED READING: *Collected Poems of Edna St. Vincent Millay* (Harper & Row).

Edna St. Vincent Millay's Poems: Selected for Young People (woodcuts by Ronald Keller; Harper & Row).

Letters of Edna St. Vincent Millay (out of print).

ARAKIDA MORITAKE (1473–1549) was a Japanese Shinto priest at the Great Shrine at Ise. He precedes even the great Japanese haiku poets Bashō and Issa, and though Bashō invented the short three-line form we know now as haiku, or hokku, many believe that Moritake's work led the way.

SUGGESTED READING: *The Classic Tradition of Haiku: An Anthology* (edited by Faubion Bowers; Dover Thrift Editions).

From the Country of Eight Islands: An Anthology of Japanese Poetry (edited and translated by Hiroaki Sato and Burton Watson; University of Washington Press).

World Within Walls: Japanese Literature of the Pre-Modern Era, 1600–1867 (by Donald Keene; Holt, Rinehart and Winston).

AMADA NERVO (1870–1919) studied for the priesthood as a young adult growing up in Mexico. Though he led an active public life as journalist and diplomat, he was known as "the Monk of Poetry." After the death of his beloved Ana Daillex, with whom he had lived for eleven years, he wrote a series of poems offering "even his grief to God." His late collections had names like *Serenity* (1914) and *Elation* (1917).

SUGGESTED READING: *The Soul-Giver* (poems translated by Gloria Schaffer Meléndez; E. Mellen Press).

Twentieth Century Latin-American Poetry: A Bilingual

Anthology (translated by Stephen Tapscott; University of Texas Press).

FRANK O'HARA (1926–1966) was born in Baltimore, Maryland. He went to Harvard with fellow poets John Ashbery and Kenneth Koch, and worked at *Art News* and at the Museum of Modern Art, starting as a lowly desk clerk, eventually becoming a key figure in the world of modern art. A true Renaissance man, he trained at the New England Conservatory of Music; championed the work of Jackson Pollock and many experimental artists; founded the Poet's Theater, and was considered the leading force in the so-called New York School of Poets (though later he moved to San Francisco), as well as an honorary member of the Beat Generation (see Allen Ginsberg). He died in an automobile accident on Fire Island in New York. O'Hara's poems are notable for their long, conversational rhythms and wild, gentle humor, sorrow, and wisdom. His work celebrates everything and everyone, from New York City streets to "having a Coke" to Billie Holiday.
SUGGESTED READING: *The Collected Poems of Frank O'Hara* (edited by Donald Allen; University of California Press).
Lunch Poems (City Lights Books).

MARY OLIVER (b. 1935) won the Pulitzer Prize in 1984 for her book of poems, *American Primitive,* and the National Book Award in 1992 for her *New and Selected Poems.* She is best known as a pastoral and nature poet, but while her work celebrates the natural and rural world it touches on much more than this suggests. One of her readers has called her "a poet of the human spirit," and another described her work as "an unmasking of the natural world." She has taught at many colleges and universities and holds the Catherine Osgood Foster Chair for Distinguished Teaching at Bennington College in Vermont.

SUGGESTED READING: *New and Selected Poems* (Beacon Press).

A Poetry Handbook (the poet's theories, definitions, and advice on the writing of poetry; Harcourt Brace).

PSALMIST: King David is traditionally credited with composing many of the psalms. Regardless of authorship, the psalms are prayer-songs that range from desperation to hope to joy and have comforted millions for three thousand years. SUGGESTED READING: The Holy Bible (any version you like best).

The Psalms (Dover Thrift Editions).

CHARLES REZNIKOFF (1894–1976) grew up in Brooklyn, New York. His parents were Russian Jews who had recently immigrated to the United States. Reznikoff graduated from the Boys' High School in Brooklyn at the age of fifteen, and by the time he was sixteen had determined to be a writer. He studied journalism at the University of Missouri for a year, left, and returned to New York to work at his parents' hat manufacturing business. He earned his law degree but actually spent very little of his life practicing law. Instead, he took on a number of jobs, wrote plays, essays, and poems, and was one of a group of poets in the 1930s to form their own press. Reznikoff's poems are remarkable for their gentle compassion, celebration of daily life, and modesty. One of his poems declares that he wrote his poetry "not for the table upon the dais, / but at the common table."
SUGGESTED READING: *By the Well of Living & Seeing: New & Selected Poems* (Black Sparrow Press).

The Complete Poems of Charles Reznikoff, volumes one and two (Black Sparrow Press).

RAINER MARIA RILKE (1875–1926) was born and raised in Prague, but spent most of his life in self-exile from his native land. He worked for a time as secretary to the great French sculptor Auguste Rodin, who taught the poet to "work, work incessantly"—advice that, given Rilke's passionate and ethereal nature, was often agony for him to follow. Although he married and had a child, he was uncomfortable in the conventional role of husband and parent. He once described an ideal partnership as "two solitudes that border and protect one another," and also wrote, "For one human being to love another; that is perhaps the hardest of all; the ultimate, the last task and proof, the work for which all other work is only preparation."

After Rilke had finished his novel, *The Notebooks of Malte Laurids Brigge,* he became so despondent, so unsure of himself, that he went through more than ten "crisis years," in which he felt himself to be living in a whirlwind of silence and failure. In fact, he was writing all along—poems, letters—but it was not until he finished his *Duino Elegies,* which he had begun twelve years earlier, that the spell was broken; that same fruitful year he wrote his *Sonnets to Orpheus.*

SUGGESTED READING: *Letters to a Young Poet* (translated by Stephen Mitchell; Vintage).

Selected Poems of Rainer Maria Rilke (translated by Robert Bly; Harper & Row).

LIZ ROSENBERG (b. 1956) grew up on the North Shore of Long Island, and has spent a great deal of her life near the sea, in New York, Florida, and New England. After attending Bennington College, she earned her master's degree at Johns Hopkins University and her doctorate in Comparative Literature at SUNY Binghamton. She has taught creative writing and English for twenty years at the State University of New York in Binghamton, where she lives with her husband, David, their son, Eli, and two shih tzu dogs. In addition to publishing two books of her own poems, she has edited three anthologies of poetry for young readers (including this one), as well as a novel, short stories, book reviews, a book of prose poems, and more than a dozen picture books. She speaks and teaches at elementary and middle schools all over the country, and has worked as a Literacy Volunteer since 1996.

SUGGESTED READING: *Children of Paradise* (by Liz Rosenberg; University of Pittsburgh Press).

Earth-Shattering Poems (edited by Liz Rosenberg; Henry Holt).

These Happy Eyes: Prose Poems (edited by Liz Rosenberg; Mammoth Press).

The Invisible Ladder: An Anthology of Contemporary American Poetry for Young Readers (edited by Liz Rosenberg; Henry Holt).

CHRISTINA ROSSETTI (1836–1894) was born in London, England, sister of the poet Dante Gabriel Rossetti. Like him, she was educated at home in their devoutly Christian family. (One sister, Maria, became a nun.) After an unhappy romance Christina wrote almost continuously, living in seclusion with her mother. Together, they tried to support the family by running a day school, which did not succeed. Christina herself was known to be extraordinarily devout, almost saintly; for instance, she gave up playing chess because she "too much enjoyed winning."

SUGGESTED READING: *Christina Rossetti: Selected Poems* (Bloomsbury Classic Poetry Series, St. Martin's Press).

These Small Stones (selected by Norma Farber and Myra Cohn Livingston; Harper & Row).

RUMI (JALAL AD-DIN MUHAMMED DINAR) (1207–1273), Persian poet and mystic, was born in what is now Afghanistan. Rumi's family escaped the advance of warring Mongols and eventually settled in what is now part of western Turkey. In 1244 Rumi met his first great love and religious guide, the mystic Shams ad-Din, a Sufi dervish master, and his life changed completely. The poems he composed—nearly thirty thousand of them—were uttered out loud, many in passionate praise of Shams (whom he calls the Friend, meaning both spiritual teacher, lover, and God). In 1247 Shams mysteriously disappeared—some believe he was murdered by jealous rivals. Later spiritual masters and loves inspired further poetry, including the epic poem *Masnavi-ye Manevi* (Spiritual Couplets). Rumi was the first whirling dervish—one who spins or dances himself into a state of spiritual ecstasy. His translator, Coleman Barks, is also a poet himself, whose own work, not surprisingly, shares some of Rumi's tender, comic, mystifying, soulful qualities.

SUGGESTED READING: *Birdsong* (fifty-three short poems translated by Coleman Barks; Maypop Press).

The Essential Rumi (translated by Coleman Barks; Harper-Collins).

Gourd Seed (poetry by Coleman Barks; Maypop Press).

KATE SCHMITT (b. 1973) grew up in New England, but spent part of her childhood in Hong Kong. She earned a bachelor's degree from Colgate University, then worked in publishing in Boston before moving back to Asia for a time, where she taught English at a university in northern China, and then moved to Houston, Texas, to attend graduate school. She has taught creative writing to elementary school children and college students, as well as teaching American literature and Chinese. She has recently finished her first novel for young readers.

SUGGESTED READING: Kate Schmitt's first published poem appeared in *Earth-Shattering Poems* (an anthology of worldwide poems for young readers; Henry Holt).

HENRY M. SEIDEN (b. 1940) is a psychologist and psychotherapist who practices in Forest Hills, New York. He has lived there with his wife and his children (now grown, with children of their own) since earning his doctoral degree in 1969 from the New School for Social Research. He has published poems in numerous journals, including *Poetry, The Humanist,* and the *Journal of the American Medical Association.* He has also coauthored a book called *Silent Grief: Living in the Wake of Suicide.* Mr. Seiden writes, "Sanity isn't a matter of good outcomes, good solutions to problems. . . . Most people's lives are more or less a muddle. What makes a difference is whether you are alive or dead in the middle of your mess. Can you think clearly? Feel deeply? Can you feel the pain? Can you get the joke?"

SUGGESTED READING: *Silent Grief: Living in the Wake of Suicide* (by Christopher Lukas and Henry M. Seiden; Jason Aronson Books.)

PERCY BYSSHE SHELLEY (1792–1822) was born in Sussex, England, and educated at Oxford. He married Harriet Westbrook, and after her suicide married Mary Wollstonecraft Godwin, the author of the famous *Frankenstein,* written when she was only eighteen. Shelley is known for his dramatic, exuberant, emotional lines, such as "I fall upon the thorns of life! I bleed!" He was extremely generous to his fellow poets in time of need, offering protection and sanctuary to Byron and also to Keats (who considered Shelley scandalous). Like so many of the Romantics, he died young, drowned in the Gulf of Spezia. In his pocket was found a copy of Keats's poems.

SUGGESTED READING: *Shelley: Poems* (Everyman's Library Pocket Poets, Knopf).

The Works of Percy Bysshe Shelley (Wordworth Editions, Ltd.).

CHRISTOPHER SMART (1722–1771), English poet and journalist, was as eccentric in his way as William Blake (a younger contemporary) was in his. Smart, however, has been treated almost entirely as a mad poet, almost an embarrassment to literature. He worked for the famous bookseller John Newbery (who also sold quack remedies, and for whom the well-known Newbery Prize in Children's Literature is named), but in 1756 what was considered a "religious mania" overtook him, and he was consigned to an asylum for the insane. While there, he wrote what one biographer has called "the incoherent poem" *Jubilate Agno* (Rejoice in the Lamb) from which "My Cat Jeoffry" is here excerpted. In it, Smart describes himself as "the Lord's News-Writer." A contemporary, Samuel Johnson wrote of him: "My poor friend Smart showed the disturbance of his mind by falling upon his knees, and saying his prayers in the street, or any other unusual place . . . it is greater madness not to pray than to pray as Smart did."

SUGGESTED READING: *My Cat Jeoffry: A Poem by Christopher Smart* (edited by Martin Leman; Penguin Books).

Christopher Smart Selected Poems (Penguin Classics).

GARY SOTO (b. 1952) was born, raised, and educated in Fresno, California. A leading writer and spokesperson among Chicanos (Mexican Americans), Soto has created more than a dozen books for children and for adults: award-winning poetry, short stories, anthologies, picture books, novels, and two documentaries filmed in Spanish. His work ranges from the comic to the heartbreaking, from gentle to furious—and everything between. A National Book Award finalist, he lives in California, where he teaches at the University of California at Berkeley.

SUGGESTED READING: *Gary Soto: New and Selected Poems* (Chronicle Books).

Junior College (Chronicle Books).

Pieces of the Heart: New Chicano Fiction (edited by Gary Soto; Chronicle Books).

Petty Crimes (short stories for young adults; Harcourt Brace).

WILLIAM STAFFORD (1914–1993) was born in Hutchinson, Kansas. As a conscientious objector during World War Two, he began his commitment to peace and honesty, and also to a lifelong habit of writing before dawn each day, which he likened to "fishing." He taught at Lewis and Clark College, and all over the world, served as consultant in poetry to the Library of Congress in 1970, and was named Oregon's Poet Laureate in 1975. He was intensely concerned with ecological issues and matters of social justice, the treatment of Native Americans, nonviolence, and humility. The poet Naomi Shahib Nye has said of William Stafford that he "befriended the earth and its citizens most generously and attentively, at the same time remaining solitary . . . intact, composed, mysterious, complete in his humble service."

SUGGESTED READING: *Stories That Could Be True: New and Collected Poems* (Harper & Row).

The Way It Is: New and Selected Poems (Graywolf Press).

Writing the Australian Crawl (University of Michigan Press).

ROBERT LOUIS STEVENSON (1850–1894) was born in Edinburgh, Scotland, and his health was frail from the time he was a child. Because of his ill health, he was often kept at home, alone, confined to his bed, and so began, as he reported later, to spend his time making up stories in his head. Stevenson wrote poems, novels, tales, essays, and plays. His first recognition as a writer came in 1883 with the publication of *Treasure Island*, quickly followed by *A Child's Garden of Verses* (1885), but his real popular success arrived with the simultaneous publications, in 1886, of *Kidnapped* and *The Strange Case of Dr. Jekyll and Mr. Hyde*. All his life,

Stevenson dreamed of exotic places, and he finally settled in Samoa with his wife and their extended family. He was honored by the Samoans as a chief, with the name Tusitala, meaning "teller of tales."

SUGGESTED READING: *A Child's Garden of Verses* has been illustrated by a number of well-loved illustrators, including Jessie Wilcox, Tasha Tudor, and Brian Wildsmith, among others. I recommend you find your own favorite, and hang on to it.

Selected Poems of Robert Louis Stevenson (edited by Angus Calder, includes "A Child's Garden of Verses" and other poems; Penguin Classics).

RUTH STONE (b. 1915), whose father was a drummer, was born in Roanoke, Virginia. She has raised three daughters, and countless numbers of those she calls "poetry daughters and sons." She has published eleven books, and is a professor of English and creative writing in Binghamton, New York. When not in Binghamton, she lives in rural Vermont, near her daughters, and with numerous beloved cats.

SUGGESTED READING: *Ordinary Words* (Paris Press).

Simplicity (Paris Press).

RABINDRANATH TAGORE (1861–1941) was the first Asian to win the Nobel Prize in Literature, and the only poet from India to be named Nobel poet laureate. He was born in Kolkota (Calcutta) to a wealthy and well-educated family, and at the age of seventeen, after accompanying his father on various expeditions and pilgrimages, was sent to England to finish his education. He founded a school for boys and later the World University in India, dividing his time between establishing the schools, teaching, lecturing, and writing poems, essays, fiction, plays, and songs. (He was also knighted, in 1915.) The Irish poet W. B. Yeats, traveling through one of the poorest regions in India, was surprised to find women in the fields singing the songs and poems of Tagore. He was (and is) a much-beloved poet and mystic in India and abroad. Yeats said of Tagore's lyrics that they "display in their thought a world I have dreamed of all my life."

SUGGESTED READING: *Fireflies* (poetry, with decorations by Boris Artzybasheff; Macmillan).

Gitanjali (the book for which Tagore won the Nobel Prize; Brandon Publishing Company).

Rabindranath Tagore: An Anthology (contains poems, essays, letters, songs, a play, a novel, and more; Griffith).

Selected Poems (Twentieth Century Classics).

DYLAN THOMAS (1914–1953) was born and raised in a seaside town of Swansea in Wales, which he beautifully describes in *A Child's Christmas in Wales*. He was a poet and performer from an early age, and also published essays, short stories, letters, notebooks, and *Under Milk Wood, A Play for Voices*, which is available on video, with Richard Burton, Elizabeth Taylor, and others. A hard liver and harder drinker, he died a mysterious and untimely death in New York City. Nonetheless he wrote in a note to his readers: "These poems, with all their crudities, doubts, and confusions, are written for the love of Man and in praise of God, and I'd be a damn' fool if they weren't." His poem "Do Not Go Gentle into That Good Night" is written in the French form called the *villanelle*, which has extremely fixed and rigorous rules; it consists of nineteen lines with two end rhymes in six stanzas. The first and third lines of the opening three-line stanza recur alternately at the end of the other stanzas, with both repeated at the close of the final quatrain (four-line stanza). "Do Not Go Gentle into That Good Night" may be the greatest example yet of the *villanelle* in the English language.

SUGGESTED READING: *The Collected Poems of Dylan Thomas 1934–1952* (New Directions).

NOTE: There are many lovely versions of Dylan Thomas's classic *A Child's Christmas in Wales*. New Directions (New York) publishes a small, pale blue paperback edition that comes with its own envelope for mailing. Look for a number of audio recordings from Caedmon (distributed through HarperCollins, New York) featuring Thomas reading his own works, and those of others, in his unmistakable, rich, sweet, Welsh incantation.

MARINA TSVETAEVA (1892–1941) was born to a wealthy family in Moscow, Russia. Her mother, a gifted musician, died of tuberculosis when she, Marina, was a teenager, and she began publishing her own poems when she was seventeen. She married Sergei Efron, and with him had two daughters and a son. During the Russian Revolution, most of the family property was seized, and she lived from then on in dire poverty. While her husband was away in 1917 serving in the White Army, their younger daughter died of starvation. She and her two remaining children joined her husband in Berlin a few years later, then moved to Paris, returning at last to Moscow in 1938. Her sister had been sent to a prison camp by the Stalin dictatorship a year earlier, and in 1938 both her eldest daughter and husband were arrested, while she was evacuated from Moscow. In 1941, in despair of her family's safety and the future of her beloved Russia, she hanged herself. In her lifetime she wrote not only poems but verse plays, essays, and memoirs. She befriended many poets of the day, including the poets Pasternak, Akhmatova, and Rilke. Despite the many tragedies of her life, Tsvetaeva was known for her passion for art and for life, and wrote: "In Russia I'll be understood better. But in the next world I'll be understood even better than in Russia."

SUGGESTED READING: *A Captive Spirit: Selected Prose* (translated by Janet Marin King; Vintage).

Art in the Light of Conscience: Eight Essays on Poetry by Marina Tsvetaeva (translated with introduction and notes by Angela Livingstone; Harvard University Press).

Selected Poems (translated by Elaine Feinstein; Penguin Books).

WALT WHITMAN (1819–1892) was born in Huntington, Long Island, New York, in a house his father had built. At age four he and his family moved to Brooklyn, where Whitman went to school until he was twelve. He worked as teacher, journalist, editor, and, perhaps most importantly, as volunteer nurse during the Civil War, where he gave out his spare change to the wounded and dying soldiers, bought them stamps and small gifts, read and wrote letters for them, and once carried a tub of ice cream from ward to ward "for a treat" for "my boys," as he called them. Whitman was something of a sentimental hack poet until his thirty-sixth year when something—no one knows quite what—transformed him, and he abruptly became the poet we know today: "of old and young, of the foolish as much as the wise, / Regardless of others, ever regardful of others." Some say he'd had an unhappy love affair; others say he'd had a mystical experience; Whitman himself tells us only that he "heard the voice of the sea." Largely unrecognized in his life, he self-published his master work, *Leaves of Grass,* on which he worked for more than forty years, from the 1850 edition to the ninth so-called deathbed edition of 1892. Though he'd had a stroke in January 1873, and was sometimes weary of "dragging this lumbering body around," he had admirers who visited him and cared about his work. The poet, he wrote in his preface to the 1855 edition of *Leaves of Grass*, judges "not as the judge judges, but as the sun falling around a helpless thing."

He also wrote that "the United States themselves are essentially the greatest poem." His contemporary Emily Dickinson claimed she'd never read him but "heard that he is disgraceful."

SUGGESTED READING: *The Essential Walt Whitman* (edited with an introduction by Galway Kinnell; Ecco Press).

The Portable Walt Whitman (edited by Mark Van Doren, contains poems, prefaces, essays, stories; Viking).

NOTE: "A Draft of Whitman," chapter nine in Lewis Hyde's book *The Gift*, is a great biographical and critical reading of Whitman (Vintage).

WILLIAM WORDSWORTH (1770–1850) grew up in the rural English lake district. After studying at Cambridge University he spent a tempestuous year in revolutionary France, where he had an affair with a Frenchwoman. After his forced return to England, he was befriended by the poet Samuel Taylor Coleridge, one of the most productive literary friendships ever formed. Wordsworth, who became poet laureate of England, changed from the liberal and experimental thinker he had been in his youth to a man who wrote poetry in praise of capital punishment. His earlier and most beloved work is about rural life, philosophy, and remembrances of childhood. Poetry was, he proposed, "emotion recollected in tranquillity." It is said that when the poet William Blake first read Wordsworth's poem "Ode on Intimations of Immortality" he became "almost hysterical with joy."

SUGGESTED READING: *Selected Poems and Prefaces by William Wordsworth* (edited by Jack Stillinger; Houghton Mifflin).

WILLIAM BUTLER YEATS (1865–1939) was a Nobel laureate and a leader in the Irish renaissance movement. He helped to found the famous Abbey Theatre in Dublin, and was interested in everything from myth to folklore to mysticism, the occult, Irish politics, and automatic writing. Though he did

finally marry, the great love of his life was Maude Gonne, a fiery Irish nationalist, actress, and beauty whom he courted for years, to little avail. He wrote not only some of the most beautiful poetry of the twentieth century but also essays, plays, stories, tales, autobiography, and philosophy. He once wrote, "It is love that impels the soul to its expressions in thought and in action" and also that "the imagination has some way of lighting on the truth that the reason has not, and . . . its commandments, delivered when the body is still and the reason silent, are the most binding we can ever know."
SUGGESTED READING: *Early Poems Unabridged* (Dover Thrift Editions).

Essays and Introductions (Collier Books/Macmillan).

Selected Poems and Two Plays of William Butler Yeats (edited and with an introduction by M. L. Rosenthal; Collier/Macmillan).